The Temple of Iconoclasts

The Temple of Iconoclasts

by

J. Rodolfo Wilcock

Translated

from

the Italian by

Lawrence Venuti

Mercury House, San Francisco

Introduction and English translation copyright © 2000 by Lawrence Venuti
Originally published as *La sinagoga degli iconoclasti*
© 1972 Adelphi Edizioni s.p.a. milano

Published in the United States by Mercury House, San Francisco, California, a non-
profit publishing company devoted to the free exchange of ideas and guided by a
dedication to literary values. Mercury House and colophon are registered trade-
marks of Mercury House, Incorporated. Visit us at www.wenet.net/~mercury.

United States Constitution, First Amendment: Congress shall make no law respecting
an establishment of religion, or prohibiting the free exercise thereof; or abridging
the freedom of speech, or of the press; or the right of the people peaceably to
assemble, and to petition the Government for a redress of grievances.

Cover art:
"The School of Athens," fresco in the Palazzo de Vaticano, Rome, by Raphael
(Raffaello Sanzio, 1483–1520). Photo credit: Erich Lessing/Art Resource, NY.

Photograph of J. Rodolfo Wilcock depicts his role as
Caiphas in *The Gospel According to St. Matthew* by Pier Paolo Pasolini.
Photo courtesy of the Fondo Pier Paolo Pasolini, Roma.
Video distributed in the U.S. by Water Bearer Films, NY.

Designed and typeset by Kirsten Janene-Nelson in Adobe Garamond
and DaVinci Forward, a font designed after the handwriting of Leonardo da
Vinci, care of the P22 Type Foundry. Additional production and editorial work
by Justin Edgar and Jeremy Bigalke, San Francisco, California.

This book has been made possible by generous support
from the National Endowment for the Arts.

Printed on acid-free paper and manufactured by
Sheridan Books, Chelsea, Michigan.

Library of Congress Cataloging-in-Publication Data:
Wilcock, Juan Rodolfo, 1919–1978.
    [Sinagoga degli iconoclasti. English]
    The temple of Iconoclasts / by J. Rodolfo Wilcock ; translated from the Italian by
Lawrence Venuti.
        p. cm.
    isbn 1-56279-119-2 (trade pbk.)
        1. Imaginary biography. I. Venuti, Lawrence. II. Title.

PQ5988.W5 S57 2000
853—dc21
                                                                            99-086599

In Memoriam

Michael Francis Venuti

aka Big Mike

Contents

J. Rodolfo Wilcock

The more I learn about him, the more intriguingly eccentric he seems. Starting with the curious name: it signals his motley cultural make-up, partly Hispanic, partly Italian, partly English. The "J" stands for "Juan."

Wilcock was born in Buenos Aires in 1919, on the 17th of April, into a family with distant Spanish connections. His father, Charles Wilcock, was English; his mother, Ida Romegialli, was Italian. Juan Rodolfo was their only child. He was sickly, anemic; eating disgusted him. He learned Spanish in London, English and Italian in Argentina, where he trained as a civil engineer.

In the 1940s Wilcock began a long association with the group of innovative writers that included Jorge Luis Borges, Adolfo Bioy Casares, and Silvina Ocampo. He contributed to their anthologies of fantastic literature (1940) and Argentine poetry (1941). They affectionately called him "Johnny." He spent a year in remote Mendoza working on the construction of a Transandean railway. Over the next two decades he wrote poetry, literary criticism, and short fiction in Spanish. He started magazines and published six books of lyric poems in a romantic, symbolist vein, some with a homoerotic subtext.

Repulsed by Juan Perón's dictatorship (1946-55), Wilcock began traveling abroad, searching for a congenial place to stage an exile. In 1954, he sojourned in England, where he worked as a commentator for the BBC and as a translator for the Central Office of Information. He returned to Argentina, however, and finally chose Italy, abandoning his mother tongue for his mother's land. In April of 1957, he told a friend (in Spanish): "I'm going to Italy to write in Italian; Castilian just doesn't do it anymore." Before Wilcock left, he scoured the bookshops in Buenos Aires, buying up all the available copies of his poetry, intent on destroying them.

He landed in Rome, where he lived alone in an unfurnished house whose walls were lined with books. Beginning in 1960 he started to publish in Italian. His first volume, *Chaos,* was a self-translation, a free Italian version of stories he wrote in Spanish some two decades earlier.

In 1962 Wilcock settled in the town of Lubriano, near Viterbo, just north of Rome. Over the next decade and a half, he produced some fifteen books in Italian: poetry, drama in verse and prose, cultural journalism, and several volumes of fiction, both novels and stories. He now associated with such leading Italian writers as Alberto Moravia, Elsa Morante, Tommaso Landolfi, and Pier Paolo Pasolini. He played the role of Caiphas in Pasolini's film *The Gospel According to St. Matthew* (1964). He wrote for various Italian periodicals, ranging from widely circulated newspapers and magazines (*Il Mondo, L'Espresso*) to avant-garde theater journals (*Sipario*). And he became an extremely prolific translator into Italian. Not only did he render the writing of his Argentine friends, he also collaborated on translations with Livio Bacchi, who became his adoptive son and heir.

A partial catalogue of Wilcock's translations reveals the dazzling range of his interests: Marlowe's plays, Shakespeare's *Richard III,* John Aubrey's *Brief Lives,* Rider Haggard's *She,* Virginia Woolf's *A Room of One's Own,* Beckett's English poetry,

J. Rodolfo Wilcock

Black Elk Speaks, Edward Dahlberg's *Because I Was Flesh,* excerpts from Joyce's *Finnegans Wake,* the collected plays of Jean Genet, *Macbird,* Flann O'Brien's *At Swim-two-birds,* William Carlos Williams's *In the American Grain.*

In 1977 Wilcock wrote to the Italian novelist Alberto Arbasino (presumably in Italian, here translated from Spanish): "I still consider myself an exile. Exiles are less depressed than everyone else. The book I'm writing is an exile's book. For everyone else, it isn't a book at all, just a series of tales disguised as literature."

In March of 1978, Wilcock suffered a fatal heart attack. He was found sitting on the sofa, alone, holding open before him a book on heart ailments.

Weighing the evidence in Buenos Aires, Silvina Ocampo insisted: "Johnny was poisoned."

FROM BIRTH, one might say, Juan Rodolfo Wilcock was deracinated, an émigré in transit between diverse languages and cultures, periods and styles. His interests were modernist. He nurtured an experimentalist's fascination with classical and Renaissance literature, the American oral tradition, pop romance, topical allegory. His writing wittily combines literary allusion, learned speculation, and fantastic inventiveness. He favored parodies and gave them a savagely satiric twist, often resorting to the grotesque.

The philosophical themes in his early work (1940s–1960s) reflected current existentialist thinking: the vagaries of human identity, determined by social relationships yet arbitrary, likely to disintegrate and transform with extreme experiences. Once Wilcock began to travel, his concept of identity exfoliated. In the fiction he published throughout the 1970s, the characters are

The Temple of Iconoclasts

both generic and historical, multiply inflected by race, gender, sexuality, and nationality, housed in various social institutions, whether academic or artistic, religious or scientific, political or commercial. Wilcock's most ambitious narrative is a metafictional exercise entitled *I due allegri indiani* (1973; A Couple of Gay Indians), wherein a western novel about two North American Indians is being serialized in a weekly horse-racing sheet. Cranky letters-to-the-editor punctuate the unfolding horse opera which is, moreover, capacious enough to contain anthropological treatises on Indians, drawing room repartee reminiscent of Ronald Firbank, and homosexual pornography.

Wilcock's fiction is carnivalesque, suffused with the dark humor that accompanies the collapse or sheer subversion of hallowed truths, official standards, institutional authority. Jacket copy he wrote for one of his books refers to the "impossibility, in our culture, of severing the tragic from the ridiculous." Wilcock's hilarotragedy takes the form of pastiche, camp, and surreal juxtapositions.

These qualities are happily displayed in *La sinagoga degli iconoclasti* (1972; The Temple of Iconoclasts). Wilcock's iconoclasts are engaged in weirdly imagined discoveries or experiments. They challenge the status quo in many fields and disciplines, including medicine, physics, politics, philosophy, literature, archaeology, pyramidology, volcanology, even lexicography. The projects are designed to bring about cultural and social change, sometimes on a global scale. Almost all of them are described in a deadpan or dryly academic tone that shifts between comic ridicule and caustic irony, at once funny and disturbing. Here Wilcock is a learned critic of the political uses to which specialized learning is sometimes put.

At times the writing recalls Eugène Ionesco's plays, particularly *The Lesson* (1951), that macabre tutorial session in which a professor browbeats a pupil into learning nonsense and finally murders her. There are also traces of a grimly amusing satirist like Jonathan Swift. Among the wonders of *Gulliver's Travels* is the island where scientists try to extract sunbeams from cucumbers and build houses from the roof down. Yet unlike the liberating anarchism of Ionesco or the misanthropic rationalism of Swift, Wilcock's own standpoint seems democratic. His zany scientists, inventors, scholars, and utopian thinkers make discoveries that reach into a range of oppressive ideologies and political agendas: religious fanaticism, commercialism, nationalism, imperialism, racism.

What makes *The Temple of Iconoclasts* compelling to read, however, is not the magnitude of the revelations, but the genre in which Wilcock chose to frame his book: the biographical sketch, especially as embodied in encyclopedia entries. He sought to erase the distinction between art and life by depicting his fantastic characters with scholarly verisimilitude. He also inserted some real people among the fictions, historical figures with an iconoclastic bent. Their projects likewise strain credibility, but these figures actually performed experiments, articulated theories in treatises, and created institutions that had an effect on the world.

As Wilcock acknowledged in his note, the chapters dedicated to real people are based on Martin Gardner's 1952 collection of pseudoscientific fads and fallacies, *In the Name of Science*. Wilcock used this meticulously researched book in a number of ways, translating, adapting, revising. Not only did he rework Gardner's incredulous yet straightforward accounts, but he set them in a new, ironical context, mixing journalism with satire, history with absurdism.

The Temple of Iconoclasts

ON THE ITALIAN LITERARY SCENE, Wilcock continues to enjoy the status of a contemporary classic, kept in print by a distinguished Milanese publisher. He also commands an international readership—in Spain, France, Argentina. His writing has never been translated into English, and there is certainly nothing quite like it in current British and American fiction, where the preference for realism remains dominant. Realism even dominates recent narrative trends that are touted as "multicultural." As a result, it threatens to replace cultural diversity with a homogeneous narrative form that fosters the illusion of ethnic realities and racial essences.

I chose to translate Wilcock precisely because he can unsettle and perhaps advance thinking about narrative and cultural identity. He exemplifies the truly international tendencies in contemporary fiction, where literary affiliations, shared forms and themes, arise from global flows of immigration and displacement, cultural exchange and assimilation. Although written in Italian in 1972, *The Temple of Iconoclasts* addresses social issues that are urgently debated in English today. It celebrates ethnic diversity while acknowledging the brutal hierarchies that have long been constructed between different ethnic groups. It also demonstrates that the consequences of diversity are highly unpredictable—and not always desirable.

There is another, more writerly reason why I chose to translate Wilcock: his style. Although the tone inclines toward scholarly detachment and the recurrent form is biography, Wilcock's remarkable invention is matched by a stylistic variety that reflects the different projects, personalities, disciplines, and aspirations of his iconoclasts. He offers his translator a rare opportunity to write with a more intense self-consciousness, to range over various dialects and discourses, conventions and genres, to play the

J. Rodolfo Wilcock

arch mimic. I soon saw that fluent translating would evoke the surreal irony hovering over each chapter. And this meant that an occasional variation would be enough to create an added ironic sense: to suggest, however vaguely, that the reader is reading a translation, not to be confused with some pure, authentic original, more like a hybrid of the domestic and the foreign, English and the polylingual materials that compose the Italian text. For how could the sheer heterogeneity of Wilcock's writing ever make it purely his?

Wilcock is infectious. The translator who catches him forever feels a strange detachment from writing, an acute sense of its irreducible otherness—despite the labor of bending it into self-expression. Like this introduction: part potted encyclopedia entry, part belles-lettres appreciation, describing a figure who belongs in a book entitled *The Temple of Iconoclasts*.

L.V.
New York City
March 1999

The Temple of Iconoclasts

José Valdés y Prom

Manila-born José Valdés y Prom became quite well known for his extraordinary powers of telepathy, especially in Paris. In this city, the center of the world, the web of his ubiquitous mind stretched its instantaneous filaments to Madrid, New York, Varsavia, and Sofia. But the spider himself had no desire to stir from his cone-shaped nest, his hyperboloid, his dirty sixth-floor apartment in rue Visconti on the Left Bank. Far more than a student of the parapsychological sciences, he died of a heart attack on the disgustingly filthy stairs, which much augmented his fame.

The French, because of their celebrated ignorance of geography as well as any language that wasn't French, took him for Japanese, Chilean, Papuan, Thai, Indian, Eskimo, Mexican, and Portuguese, in accordance with current trends and events. His simple double surname likewise underwent metamorphoses worthy of an Egyptian pharaoh whose name is usually recognized only by the first, second, or last letter. He signed *Ramses* only to avoid *Sesostris*.

This explains why the great medium is remembered in Rome under the name of Giuseppe Valdez, in Vienna as Joss von Yprom, in London as J.V. Bromie, and among the Gnostic circles of Zurich as the improbably dubbed Jonathan Waldenpromer. In 1875, two Torinese contessas, at once parsimonious and fond of spiritualism, were beggared by one of his false twins—Brescian, and blond to boot—who introduced himself as Giosuè Valdes di Promio. His fame, like that of Buddha and Jehovah, transcended orthography.

This fame was born, so to speak, with the Third Republic. In 1872, Valdés y Prom played his first telepathic game of chess with the Anabaptist minister L.B. Rumford of Tunbridge Wells—and won. The accounts of this memorable game are highly divergent. It is almost certain that the two players opened the game at the same time on the same day. What isn't clear is the fact, apparently documented, that the Englishman conceded on a Tuesday while the player in Paris didn't checkmate him till Thursday. In any case, the moves and other details of the game can be read in the *Edinburgh Review,* which demonstrates the far-flung interest in the event.

In the months and years that followed, Valdés y Prom won games through telepathy in every European capital reached by telegraph. He also played in Lublin, but unfortunately the outcome was lost in the transdanubian fog (Lublin had yet to be equipped with a telegraph system). These games were, however, extremely elementary. Valdés's competitors seemed to allow their pieces to be captured in less than no time, and the suspicion arose that the clairvoyant deliberately chose opponents who didn't know how to play chess. This suspicion diminished not a whit the value of his achievement. One need only ponder the infinite complexity of the game—which grows doubly infinite when neither player has the slightest idea of his opponent's moves. Even to lose in such circumstances is tantamount to victory.

In the interval, Valdés became the Mahatma of psychics, official finder of lost jewels and children, soothsayer to amorous field marshals, comforter of the widows of the Electors Palatine.

Exactly what he did with the enormous sums he earned no one ever knew. Some whispered that the Maestro was financing the construction of a private pyramid near Memphis in Egypt. Others asserted that he dispatched every franc to China, an idea that seemed sufficiently mysterious at the time to obviate the need for further explanation. The malicious and the obtuse affirmed—without proof, as usual—that he spent his earnings in the most opulent whorehouses in Paris, among Algerian and Tonkinese women, when they weren't Tonkinese and Algerian.

The fact is that Valdés y Prom now bore such a close resemblance to a saint as to repress any association with bordellos. It was even said that he brought back to life a delivery boy who was horribly crushed by horse-drawn tram. It was known with certainty that he hypnotized the Czar's son long-distance, during a journey to Odessa, and in this state compelled him to contact Petersburg, requesting leniency for a famous anarchist from Vladivostok who was condemned to die. But perhaps the request for leniency was simply the price he arranged with the seer in return for some other—unknown—feat. It was also confirmed that nearly every evening the Filipino threw open the window of his room, climbed on the sill, and started to stroll the length of rue Visconti, moving in the air at the height of the sixth floor, wearing a meek, reflective expression on his face. After thirty minutes' diversion he returned home through the same window. These were his only verifiable comings and goings.

At a certain point, a friend of his, a Spanish exile reduced to poverty by the Carlist wars, wished to turn a profit from the Maestro's telepathic powers by opening an information bureau—what we would today call a wire service—inside the Hôtel de Ville. Three times each week the friend climbed the stairs on rue Visconti, and the entranced Filipino cast his radar gaze over the capitals of the civilized world. This was the first modern wire service in the sense that it circulated news concerning heads of state and their normal daily activities. For example:

ROME, MARCH 17—The Pope celebrated his eighty-second birthday by saying Mass in the Sistine Chapel.

BERLIN, JUNE 6—The Iron Chancellor dedicated a bronze statue to the Prussian nation.

MONTREUX, DECEMBER 7—The suitcase belonging to the queen of Naples has been recovered.

The times were not yet sophisticated enough for this kind of high-level journalism, and the service failed. From Valdés Europe expected much greater thrills.

These were finally granted in 1878 on the occasion of the huge International Conference of Metaphysical Sciences, which unfolded, or should have unfolded, with solemn pomp in the lecture halls of the Sorbonne. Yet the Sorbonne didn't wish to be officially associated with a mass demonstration of progressive conservatism. In reality, however, the venerable institution (with its left hand) supported and even financed this gathering, which was probably planned in secret by the doubtful alliance between the still powerful Church in France and the increasing power of Scientific Materialism in Europe.

In the conciliatory climate of the new republican constitution, conflicting interests met at the conference. The Church didn't want—had never wanted—to surrender the gift of performing miracles to private citizens, as regrettably came to pass with the vote. Positivist science, more simply, didn't want any miracles to exist. Since Valdés y Prom was the only person in Paris, perhaps in Europe, whose miraculous powers were recog-

nized by all, one wouldn't be wrong to suspect that the real target
of the conference was precisely he, Valdés. Eminent theologians,
cardinals, and bishops were to unite, for once at least, with the
leading figures in physics and chemistry, even the irrepressible
evolutionists, in order to crush those muddy manifestations of
the spirit which were then called metaphysical: hypnotism,
telepathy, spiritualism, levitation. Valdés, for his part, had resolved to crush both conference and conferees without leaving
his home.

From the very first day, things took a troubling turn. The
archbishop of Paris, who was responsible for opening the event,
instead opened his big mouth and started to sing the "Rappel
des Vaches" in Savoyard patois, a song intended to summon
cows back to the barn. The prelate in fact hailed from the High
Savoy. The illustrious Ashby, a name in English science, was
scheduled to speak immediately afterward. Deeply moved, he instead lifted his hoarse mathematician's voice to intone the stro-
phes of "God Save the Queen"—every strophe, which happens
only on grand occasions.

When the applause subsided, the well-known Bohemian astronomer took the floor to announce in deplorable German that
he hadn't the foggiest idea of why they were there. No sooner did
the interpreters translate this communication for the French and
the other monolinguals present than an insistent babble inun-
dated the assembly. With reluctance at first, with triumph thereafter, everyone admitted, in the most diverse languages, that they
didn't know what they were doing there.

The proceedings were suspended, at least for the day, so that
the conference participants might return to their hotels and rec-
tories to organize their papers and thoughts. The exit from the
Great Hall was tumultuous. Struck by an almost hysterical wave
of collective glossolalia, scientists and monsignors headed for the

doors in song. The eldest burst into the carmagnole, the not-so-old into a popular new tune on the international scene. It was revived several years later by Degeyter and Pottier under the appropriate title of the "Internationale."

After his superhuman effort, Valdés y Prom was seized by a deep sleep that lasted nearly till midnight. When he awoke, he had a bit to eat, took his usual walk past the garrets on rue Visconti, and girded himself to confront the labors of the second day.

The second day of the conference *against* the Metaphysical Sciences (which, through a curious metathesis, are currently called metapsychical) was opened by the president of the Commission on Weights and Measures. He proposed that the assembly issue en masse into the courtyard to dance a polonaise in honor of Allan Forest Law, a botanist and dean at Yale in exotic Connecticut. The bishop of Caen protested that it was raining, and that the lecture hall contained sufficient space to dance a waltz. The German scientists, among whom was the rector of the University of Jena, suddenly improvised a ländler, raising a deafening racket with their clogs on the wooden floor. Gradually they were joined by the most famous geologists, volcanologists, seismologists, entomologists, and Mariologists of the period. The gathering was visibly degenerating, and this meeting too had to be adjourned. The press, which hadn't been admitted to the proceedings, could nonetheless ascertain the uproar from outside and subsequently noted the shocking heap of broken seats.

It is pointless to observe here what everybody observed then: never had anything like this happened at a scientific conference. Someone started to utter, sotto voce, the name of Valdés. Valdés y Prom received neither journalists nor correspondents; he didn't release statements. The fear arose that he had something much more devastating in reserve.

The Papal nuncio, concerned for the prestige of the clergy involved, asked to participate personally in the third day of the conference. As soon as Valdés learned of this development (thanks to the Spanish exile, who hadn't abandoned his job of collecting and transmitting news), he decided to avail himself of this massively authoritative presence (even more authoritative than the previously announced appearances of the Minister of the Interior and the Chief of Police). He would now hurl the definitive blow at his enemies.

When the nuncio entered the hall the following morning, all the participants, including Lutherans, Russians, and Turks, rose to their feet respectfully and clapped. As the applause faded, they returned to their seats. The nuncio opened his little mouth and said: "Humbly I offer you the fatherly greeting of His Holiness, the stronghold that can forever withstand demons, witches, and advocates of the sciences, whether manifest or occult." The physiologist Pukhnanov then stood up and responded: "I, Valdés y Prom, offer him mine." Sir Francis Marbler rose and added: "I, Valdés y Prom, salute the Pope." Von Statten got to his feet and said: "I, Valdés y Prom, thank the Sovereign Pontiff." One after another, every scientist stood up and expressed his gratitude in the name of the Filipino seer; then the theologians and ecclesiastics did the same. The nuncio thought he was dreaming when the Minister of the Interior finally rose and with the unmistakable accent of a Toulouse native concluded: "I, Valdés y Prom, have never been so honored."

After which all the participants moved to declare the conference closed. Unanimously, they seconded their own motion and voted their approval. Utter confusion ensued (which has been variously described) because everyone present still believed they were Valdés y Prom. With the exception of the nuncio, who, however, never discussed with anyone what actually happened that day in the Great Hall of the Sorbonne.

As if in a dream, scientists and priests alike headed for the Gare de Lyon, the Gare de Strasbourg, and their own carriages. Unable to obtain any information from them—"They acted like children," reported *La Liberté*—the journalists rushed to rue Visconti. But they couldn't learn anything else about the incident because Valdés y Prom was dead. It seems that the hypnotist was much too exhausted by the strain, and in the course of his nightly aerial stroll before the sixth floor windows, he took a step in the void, plummeting ruinously to the pavement. As for the Spanish exile, perhaps worried about possible reprisals from the Ministry of the Interior, he disappeared.

Jules Flamart

In 1964 Jules Flamart went to press with his dictionary-novel, which he shrewdly entitled *La Langue en action*. The idea was simple, but brilliant. Since standard modern lexicons, however diverting or licentious, are all unsuited to sustained, systematic reading—the factor that alone justifies the continued existence of a given work—the author proposed to compile, with Flaubertian patience, a new type of dictionary that wed the utilitarian to the adventurous. It would provide the definition and usage of each word, like a garden-variety dictionary, and yet be accompanied, not by the polite pleasantries and erudite divagations that lighten (or used to lighten) the old encyclopedias, but by brief narrative passages so linked that the diligent reader not only learns the correct use of every word in the language, but enjoys an intricately unfolding plot whose busyness rivals its naughtiness—i.e., the sort of plot usually found in pornographic spy novels.

Of course, the foregoing description is insufficient to give a fair idea of the work, which is probably unique in the world yet strangely neglected. It will be necessary, therefore, to present an excerpt, selected at random from its 850 pages, although with the intention of denying that the dictionary is a dictionary, after all, and a French one as well.

11

Let us open to page 283:

enfoncer: TO THRUST DEEPLY INTO; TO PENETRATE. Arthur *enfonça* her.

enforcir: TO REINVIGORATE. "The president's television speech will *enforci* him," observed the witty Ben Saïd.

enfouir: TO BURY; TO STASH. When Géraldine opened her eyes again, she protested, not without irony: "But where have you *enfoui* it?"

enfourcher: TO STICK WITH A PITCHFORK; TO PIERCE. "You should rather say *enfourchi*," explained the subprefect's secretary between mouthfuls of baba au rhum.

enfourchure: CROTCH. "Alastair, grab him by the *enfourchure* and try to pull him back," implored Fauban.

enfourner: TO PUT IN THE OVEN; TO BOOK. "Not for nothing do they call him the *enfourneur*," added the phony nun with an air of authority.

enfreindre: TO SHATTER; TO VIOLATE. "Do you like Benjamin Britten?" asked Ben Saïd, suddenly *enfreignant* the respectful silence.

enfroquer: TO PUT ON A MONK'S COWL; TO MASQUERADE AS A MONK. Beyond the door a chilling voice could be heard shouting, "*Enfroquez* him!"

enfuir (s'): TO FLEE; TO ESCAPE; TO LEAK OUT. Géraldine parted her knees and let him *s'enfouir*.

enfumer: TO SMOKE; TO FILL OR STAIN WITH SMOKE. Slipping the secretary's panties over his head in the guise of eyeglasses, Alastair *enfuma* them with his peculiar huffing and puffing and then lay down beside her.

engadine: ENGADINE. She reeked of *engadine*.

engagé: HIRED. "Why that hangdog *engagé* look?" the little nun asked him sarcastically as she threw herself into the armchair, on Fauban's lap, and stretched her right foot toward the button.

engageant: ATTRACTIVE; PREPOSSESSING. The door suddenly opened, and Géraldine saw a not very *engageant* Saint Bernard enter the room.

engagement: PLEDGE; PROMISE. The nurse who was following Ben Saïd suddenly pounced on him. "I have kept my *engagement*," she announced, smiling ambiguously, and with a swift gesture she thrust the needle of a huge hypodermic syringe into his left ear.

Ⓞ R ELSE TAKE PAGE 577:

personne: PERSON; ANYONE; NO ONE. The captain entered the shaft and said: *"Personne!"*

personnellement: PERSONALLY. The aspiring parachutist dared to advance a timid objection: "I, *personnellement*—" The other man hissed and darted out his tongue. "Wearing nothing but those flimsy pants, cut out of the evening newspaper?"

perspective: PERSPECTIVE. "That's a matter of *perspective*," bellowed the boy. "Yours, however, are made of cheap silk."

perspicace: PERSPICACIOUS; SHREWD. "You're *perspicace*," observed the captain, shoving him into the darkness.

perspiration: SLOW TRANSPIRATION. Michel was drenched in *perspiration.*

persuader: TO PERSUADE. Something in the loud tinny noise at the end of the corridor didn't *persuadait* him.

persuasion: PERSUASION. But suddenly, on his delicately haired leg, he felt the slippery barrel of a pistol, and then a silent hand, coldly determined to brush aside any compromise to its work of *persuasion.*

persulfure: PERSULPHATE. The stench of *persulfure* assailed them.

perte: LOSS; WASTE. "And this?" the officer finally asked, without releasing his victim. "Is this a *perte?*"

pertinace: PERSISTENT. La Condamine's colleagues in Counterespionage—not to mention her numerous enemies in intelligence agencies around the world—knew very well how *pertinace* she could be.

pertinent: APT; RELEVANT. "Do you really think that's a *pertinent* question?" said the boy, removing his hand from his nose and immediately stripping off his undershirt. "It belongs to me," he added, "and I'm keeping it to myself."

pertuis: HOLE; OPENING; PERFORATION. "It really isn't so large," mumbled the officer. "Here's the *pertuis!*" he abruptly exclaimed, licking his moustache.

perturbation: PERTURBATION. The neophyte's perspiration metamorphosed into *perturbation.*

péruvien: PERUVIAN. "Do you hear that tinny noise down there?" whispered his guide. "It's the *péruviens.*"

pervers: PERVERSE. "They say they're terribly *pervers!*" murmured the adolescent with a shudder.

pervertir: TO PERVERT; TO DEPRAVE. Without making the slightest move to detach himself, the captain dragged Michel two more meters into the dark tunnel. "Worse still," he said between his teeth, "they're *pervertis!*"

pesage: WEIGHING; THE WEIGH-IN. And with an absent-minded air he proceeded to the *pesage.*

pesant: HEAVY. "Do you find him *pesant?*" asked the boy, suddenly inquisitive.

pessaire: PESSARY. "Shit," La Condamine blurted out, "I've left the *pessaire* in the Jaguar-Morris."

pessimisme: PESSIMISM. A new stench, more violent than the first, swept away his *pessimisme.* This time it was a question of a public lavatory, probably communicating with a cinema.

peste: PLAGUE; THE DEUCE! DAMN IT! "Here we are," he said. *"Peste!"* exclaimed Michel. "How am I going to dry myself?"

Jules Flamart

AND SO FORTH till the blazing finale, which turns on an orgy of *zythum* (zythos), ale of the ancients and particularly the Egyptians. Didactically impeccable, especially suitable for young people and students in general, Flamart's work is one of those dictionaries—so rare, alas!—that compel breathless, nonstop reading from the first to the last page, dictionaries born with the sign of epic on their brow.

Aaron Rosenblum

Utopians are heedless of methods. To render the human species happy, they are prepared to subject it to murder, torture, lethal injection, incineration, deportation, sterilization, quartering, lobotomy, electrocution, military invasion, bombing, etc. Everything depends on the project. Somehow it is encouraging to think that even in the absence of a project, men are and always will be prepared to murder, torture, sterilize, quarter, bomb, etc.

Aaron Rosenblum, born in Danzig, raised in Birmingham, also resolved to bring happiness to humanity. The injuries he caused were not immediate. He published a book on the topic, but the book long lay neglected, so he garnered few adherents. If he had enjoyed a following, in all likelihood Europe would now be without a single potato, street light, ballpoint pen, piano, or condom.

Aaron Rosenblum's idea was extremely simple. He wasn't the first to think it, but the first to pursue it to its utmost consequences. Only on paper, however, since humanity does not always desire to do what it must to be happy. Or it prefers to choose its own methods, which, as with the best global projects, also entail murder, torture, imprisonment, exile, germ warfare, drug therapies. Chronologically, Rosenblum's utopia was unfortunate. The book destined to bring him fame, *Back to Happiness, or Joyride to Hell*, appeared in 1940, precisely when the intellec-

17

tual world was busily engaged in defending itself from another, equally utopian project of social reform, total reform.

Rosenblum first asked himself: What was the happiest period of world history? Believing himself English, and as such the trustee of a well-defined literary tradition, he decided that the happiest historical period was the magnificently exciting reign of Elizabeth I, under the sage guidance of Lord Burghley. Or at least this was the moment when Shakespeare emerged, England discovered America, and the Catholic Church was forever defeated and forced to seek refuge in the remote Mediterranean. Rosenblum had himself been a High Church Anglican for many years.

Hence, the project of *Back to Happiness* was this: to return the world to 1580. To abolish coal, machines, engines, the electric light, corn, petroleum, film, asphalt streets, newspapers, the United States, airplanes, the vote, gasoline, parrots, motorcycles, the Rights of Man, tomatoes, steamships, the iron and steel industry, the pharmaceutical industry, the Eiffel Tower, Newton and gravitation, Milton, Dickens, and Mickey Mouse, turkeys, surgery, railroads, aluminum, museums, anilines, guano, celluloid, Belgium, dynamite, the weekend, the Seventeenth Century, the Eighteenth Century, the Nineteenth Century, the Twentieth Century, mandatory education, iron bridges, the bus, light artillery, disinfectants, coffee. Tobacco could remain, seeing that Sir Walter Raleigh smoked.

By the same token, it was necessary to reestablish: debtors' prison; the gallows for thieves; slavery for blacks; the stake for witches; ten years of compulsory military service; the custom of abandoning babies by the road at birth; torches and candles; the practice of dining in a hat with a knife; the use of the rapier, cutlass, and poniard; hunting with bows; brigandage in the woods;

persecution of the Jews; the study of Latin; the prohibition against women appearing on the stage; buccaneers attacking Spanish galleons; the use of the horse for transport and the ox for motor power; bearbaiting; the institution of primogeniture; the Maltese Knights at Malta; scholastic logic; the plague, smallpox, and typhus as forms of population control; respect for nobility; mud puddles in central urban streets; wooden buildings; blood-letting; swans breeding on the Thames and hawks in castles; alchemy as a pastime; astrology as a science; the institution of vassalage; trial by ordeal; the lute indoors, the trumpet in the open air; tournaments, damascened armor, coats of arms; the chamber pot—in a word, the past.

Now it was obvious, even in Rosenblum's eyes, that the planning and ordered realization of such a utopia in 1940 would require time and patience, beyond the enthusiastic collaboration of the most influential segment of public opinion. Adolf Hitler, it is true, seemed disposed to facilitate the most compelling aspects of the project, especially those involving eliminations. Yet like a good Christian Aaron Rosenblum could not but notice that the German head of state was letting himself get too carried away by tasks that were ultimately secondary, like the suppression of the Jews and the military domination of Europe, instead of seriously applying himself to staving off the Turks, for example, or spreading syphilis, or illuminating missals.

Furthermore, however much Hitler lent the English a helping hand, he seemed secretly to nurture a certain hostility toward them. Rosenblum realized that he would have to do everything by himself—mobilize public opinion, solicit signatures and support from scientists, sociologists, ecologists, writers, artists, and, in general, lovers of the past. Unfortunately, three months after the publication of the book, the author was recruited by the

Home Guard to watch over a warehouse of absolutely no importance in the most deserted area on the Yorkshire coast. He didn't even have a telephone at his disposal. His utopia ran the risk of foundering.

It was he who foundered, however, and in a most unusual manner. As he wandered down the beach, gathering cockles and other sixteenth-century items for lunch, he was killed in an air raid apparently performed as an exercise, blown to pieces in a pit. His remains were immediately swallowed by the sea.

Mention has already been made of the utopians' lethal vocation. The bomb that destroyed Rosenblum also bespoke a utopia, not very different from his, even if in appearance more violent. Essentially, his project was based upon the progressive rarefaction of the present. Starting not with Birmingham, which was too dirty and would have required at least a century of cleaning, but with a small provincial town like Penzance, it was simply a question of delimiting a zone—perhaps acquiring it with funds from the yet-to-be-founded Sixteenth Century Society—and excluding, with the most fastidious resolve, each and every thing, custom, style, musical composition, disease, and word dating back to the incriminated centuries, that is, XVII, XVIII, XIX, and XX. A fairly complete list of excluded objects, concepts, events, and phenomena fills four chapters in Rosenblum's book.

At the same time, the sponsoring institution, namely the Sixteenth Century Society, would provide for the reintroduction of the aforementioned (brigands, candles, swords, codpieces, beasts of burden, and so forth, through another four chapters of the book). And this would be sufficient to convert the nascent colony into a paradise, or something very similar to a paradise. From London people would hasten in throngs to take the plunge into the 1500s—to wear doublets and ruffs, to crack nuts at the Globe Theatre, to empty their chamber pots into the open sewers. The resulting filth would immediately initiate a process of natural selection, necessary to reduce the population to 1580 levels.

With the contributions of visitors and new members, the Sixteenth Century Society would find itself in a position to enlarge its field of action gradually, expanding even as far as London. Sweeping four centuries of houses and iron manufactures from the capital was a problem requiring a separate solution, probably the announcement of a competition for projects open to all young lovers of the past. The other utopian, the One-Across-the-Channel, seemed already to have something like this in mind. In doubt, Rosenblum opted for encircling: perhaps a mere cincture of Sixteenth Century around London would suffice to precipitate a total collapse.

The project then proceeded rapidly to cover all of England, and from England Europe. In reality, the two utopians were heading for the same goal by different paths: to insure the happiness of humankind. Hitler's utopia, meanwhile, fell into that extreme discredit with which everyone is familiar. Rosenblum's, in contrast, resurfaces periodically in different guises: some favor the Middle Ages, others the Roman Empire, still others the State of Nature, and Greenblatt even favors the return of the Ape. If the estimated population of the chosen period were subtracted from current figures for the world, one would find that billions of people, or hominids, were condemned to death, in accordance with the project. These proposals flourish; Rosenblum's spirit continues to wander the globe.

Charles Wentworth Littlefield

With the mere force of his will, the surgeon Charles Wentworth Littlefield succeeded in making table salt crystallize into the shapes of chickens and other small animals.

Once, when his brother sustained a deep cut in his foot, which bled profusely, Dr. Littlefield got the idea of reciting a passage from the Bible, and the hemorrhage immediately stopped. From that day onward Littlefield was capable of executing the risky interventions of major surgery, adopting as a coagulant his own mental power assisted by the same Biblical excerpt.

At a certain point, the doctor decided to devote more methodical study to the secret cause of his thromboplastic power. Littlefield suspected that the salt content of blood provoked coagulation. Consequently, he dissolved a pinch of table salt in water and put the solution under the microscope. As soon as the water evaporated, the observer softly repeated the surgical passage from the Old Testament while simultaneously contemplating a chicken. Much to his surprise, he witnessed the tiny crystals slowly forming on the slide and arranging themselves into the shape of a chicken.

He repeated the experiment a hundred times, always with the same result. If, for example, he thought of a flea, the crystals settled into the shape of a flea. Littlefield reported his research in a 656-page book, *The Beginning and Way of Life* (Seattle, 1919), privately published in an edition of one hundred thousand copies. It is a profound study of the "subtle magnetism" that renders crystals docile to the control of the human mind. In the preface, the author thanks St. Paul, St. John the Evangelist, and the English physicist Michael Faraday for dictating entire chapters to him from the other world.

Aram Kugiungian

Innumerable are the believers in the transmigration of souls. Of these, not a few have proven themselves capable of remembering their previous lives or even several reincarnations. Yet one man alone maintains, not simply that he lived, but that he lives, at any precise moment, in many bodies. Foreseeably, the largest number of these bodies belong to well-known people, some quite well-known, and this fact rendered him particularly famous in narrow circles, esoteric as well as Canadian.

He was called Aram Kugiungian. As a child, he fled Turkish Armenia with his father, who was obliged to join a rather well-heeled brother in Rioja, Argentina. Yet through a fortuitous concurrence of circumstances, they instead caught up with a very poor uncle, actually a tatterdemalion, in the vicinity of Toronto. The uncle got them a ride on a vegetable cart bound for the city, where Aram's father, as he was wont to do at Erzerum, immediately went to work in a cobbler's shop.

The shoes in that country were so different from their Turkish counterparts that his only qualification for practicing the primitive craft was virtually the habit of remaining seated before a shoe. Mr. Kugiungian possessed a limited idea of the real dimensions of America, but he quickly grew weary of asking which train would take him to Rioja. Both father and son learned a simulacrum of English. Aram was disconcerted by the fact that people could be Jewish, Turkish, and Christian simultaneously. This astonishment pushed him from the agnosticism he originally held towards theosophy. The plurality that others attributed to him planted deep roots which one day would send forth unexpected branches. In the meantime he frequented a Toronto-based group known as "The Karma Wheel."

One April evening in 1949, on the sidewalk of a dirty street heading toward Lake Ontario, Aram Kugiungian first noticed that he was also someone else or, indeed, several others. He was then twenty-three years old. He hadn't finished learning English; in fact, there were girls who claimed he spoke French. America was undoubtedly a continent suited to being different people at the same time.

His father managed only to be his father, dedicated to accumulating minute sums of money inside an old victrola, whereon he laid his pillow at night. His father's uncle, however, chose not to be anyone, or more exactly, he was no one, since he hadn't made another appearance in more than a decade.

As for Aram Kugiungian, the wheel of his karma began to spin uncontrollably, as it seemed, perhaps to arrive prematurely at its fixed terminus. The fact is that at intervals of approximately every two months Aram was born again, while continuing to live in other bodies. Obviously, arithmetic is useless with souls: a soul divided by a thousand always yields a thousand perfect souls, just as the Breath of the Creator divided by three billion yields three billion Breaths of the Creator. Aram knew he was the Armenian boy of whom it was said: he wished to know who he might be.

He sought advice from his friends in the Karma Club. He made clear that he wasn't suffering from a case of double or multiple personality; he knew nothing at all about the other people. There were just occasions when, seeing a name or photograph in a newspaper or publicity poster, he experienced the acute sensation of being that person as well, whoever it might be. These abrupt encounters had already happened with a young actress, apparently English, named Elizabeth Taylor; with a Catholic archbishop from New York on a visit to Québec; and with a certain Chiang Kai-Shek, who was clearly Chinese. He didn't know whether he should contact these people, even by letter, to explain that they were all his reincarnations.

His friends were quick to understand a case of this kind, although it was the first to occur in Toronto. They listened to him with interest, with wonder, and with the respect that the supernatural inspires when it departs from its usual daily routine. They told him that if he wrote a letter to himself, he risked getting no response. So they counseled him to read the newspapers more often to see whether he could trace his identity in other people and compile a list of them for publication in the Club's monthly bulletin.

The bulletin, like the Club, was entitled *The Karma Wheel*. In the October 1949 issue, an enthusiastic note by a certain Alan H. Seaborn commented on the singular velocity of Kugiungian's soul. In addition to the above-cited people, the list of his previous incarnations (he didn't recognize the subsequent ones, probably children too young to be famous) comprised Louis de Broglie, Mossadek, Alfred Krupp, Eleanor Roosevelt, Olivier Eugène Prosper Charles Messiaen, Chaim Weitzmann, Lucky Luciano, Ninon Vallin, Stafford Cripps, Eva Perón's mother, Vladimir D'Ormesson, Lin Pao, Arturo Toscanini, Tyrone Power, El-Said Mohammed Idris, Coco Chanel, Vyacheslav Mikhailevic Molotov, Ali Khan, Anatole Litvak, Marshall Tito, John George Haigh,

Yehudi Menuhin, Ellinor Wedel (Miss Denmark), Joe Louis, and many other personalities who have since sunk into oblivion (the vampire John George Haigh, meanwhile, had been hanged in England).

His fellow club members often asked him how it felt to be so many people at the same time. Kugiungian always replied that he didn't feel anything extraordinary; in fact, he didn't feel anything at all, or at the most a vague sense of not being alone in the world. In reality, his corporal multiplicity came to be the first refutation of the so-called solipsistic thesis *in corpore vili*. Kugiungian, however, thought that Berkeley was a cricket field near Hamilton, and solipsism a form of refined vice. Several of his fellows questioned the strange coincidence that all of his simultaneous reincarnations were prominent figures. But Kugiungian prudently countered that in all likelihood his epiphanies were very frequent, and so, lacking the means to inquire into the little known, he was forced to limit himself to the most conspicuous.

At this point, a young Steinerian advanced the hypothesis that perhaps Aram Kugiungian might be the entire world population, which in that period was rather enormous. The idea was seductive—a freewheeling soul can complete a great number of revolutions per second—and Kugiungian was flattered by it. But here he had to confront the resolute opposition of the other club members, nearly all of whom obstinately refused to think of themselves as the Armenian's embodiment, whether as a reincarnation or a preincarnation. Only one young lady responded favorably to the proposal. The others took this gesture for what it certainly was, an awkward effort to flirt, on the pretext of being soul mates.

Nonetheless, Kugiungian continued to recognize himself in newspaper photographs and, later, television. From one of his statements in the *Journal of Theosophy* we must infer that ten years later, namely in 1960, apart from the above-cited people, he had also become A.J. Ayer, Dominguín, Mehdi Ben Barka, Adolf Eichmann, Princess Margaret, Karl Orff, Raoul-Albin-Louis Salan, Sir Julian Huxley, the Dalai Lama, Aram Khachaturian, Caryl Chessman, Fidel Castro, Max Born, Sygman Rhee, Elvis Presley, and Anita Ekberg.

He currently lives in Winnipeg; and although in recent years he has multiplied himself exponentially, he has never wished to meet any of his incarnations in person. Many of them do not speak English, others seem to be very busy, and, to tell the truth, he wouldn't know what to say to himself.

Theodor Gheorghescu

Ill-advised reading and a surplus of faith induced the evangelical minister Gheorghescu to preserve in salt numerous Afro-Brazilians of every age. It was calculated that the capacious tanks on his *fazenda* O Paraiso, which bordered the abandoned saltworks of Ambao outside Belém in the state of Pará, contained 227 corpses at various stages of putrefaction, all oriented in the (presumed) direction of Jerusalem. Each clenched in its teeth a herring as pickled as the deceased.

Why the Romanian minister conducted his preservation experiments in an equatorial land, where corpses were difficult to preserve, can be quickly stated. Belém is the Portuguese name for the fabled birthplace of the Savior, Bethlehem; and Gheorghescu did not realize that the guests in his tanks were corpses, since they were alive when put there. He believed them to be no more than baptized, as indicated by the fish in their mouths, symbol of Christ—baptized, that is to say, at the moment of immersion and lovingly maintained in suspended animation.

The minister actually seems never to have doubted the virtue of his deeds, regarding them instead as a modest personal contribution to the tidiness and decorum of the Last Judgment. At least *his* Africans, reasoned Theodor Gheorghescu, would come before the sight of God in good condition, neither mummies nor skeletons, nor tinned meat, nor bodies incinerated and reassembled with difficulty, but rather whole men or babies or matrons, flawless. Indeed, to all intents and purposes, they were still living. Like Saint Thomas, Gheorghescu asked himself what would happen at the Judgment to those human bodies that had been eaten and assimilated into a second body which in turn was eaten by a third and so on *ad infinitum*. Aggrieved, he tried to imagine the complicated final destiny of certain little known tribes from the interior who fancied fabulous costumes.

The humans under his protection, however, were all Africans. He would not allow an Indian into his tanks so as to avoid any mix-ups, but also in case the legends might hold a modicum of truth. Neither would he allow whites, nor even mulattos, because the minister humbly believed, just as he learned in his correspondence missionary course, that the superior race was black. Transferred in his pristine European ignorance from Constance on the Black Sea to Buenos Aires, he was astonished to observe that the southern metropolis, despite its boundless, nay, infinite expanse, didn't possess any Africans, neither savages nor any of the converted. It was rather he, a poor Romanian, who ran the risk of instruction and conversion. From a hotel for immigrants he was dispatched to an elementary school for immigrants directed by a Mormon minister.

Nauseated, Gheorghescu was soon transferred to Montevideo, a less important city but almost as unconvertible, since like Buenos Aires it was inhabited by people hostile to religions of any kind, all employed by the state. There for the first time he heard talk of Pará, which was now called Belém, hence the cradle of Our Lord as well as people of every color, ranging from red to green to black.

Twenty years passed. The minister now led a church, dedicated like him to Jehovah's Witnesses. He also owned a huge import-export firm, a hippodrome (which he never visited), a roller-skating rink (which he did), and two hundred hectares of red earth, good only for making bricks, next to the salt mines. In his Bible he wrote two Spanish sentences: "Lord, You shall see me commanding the most perfect of Your hosts. And they will be black like You."

Gheorghescu chose his candidates for the Last Act from the unemployed who lazed on the benches at his gate. If he transported any to Ambao in his orange metalflake '57 Chevy, he deposited them near the cement tanks, gave each a heavy blow to the head, performed the baptism with salt water, inserted a herring, gently laid the newly christened beside the others on a layer of dry salt, and finally coated them with more salt. The humidity quickly dissolved the salt into brine.

On the 23rd of August 1963, a servant, dismissed for a theft of herring, denounced Gheorghescu to the Brazilian police. Thus it also came to light that the minister had used one of the tanks to pickle scores of cattle, notwithstanding the possible controversy over their participation in the Resurrection of the Flesh.

Aurelianus Götze

The frivolously Christian climate that accompanied the social and political upheavals of the French Revolution precipitated a return to paganism throughout Europe. Aurelianus Götze, however, entertained a vaguer hypothesis, already proposed by the young Kant in his *Allgemeine Naturgeschichte und Theorie des Himmels* (Universal Natural History and Theory of the Heavens). To wit: the birth of the solar system resulted from the condensation of an originary nebula wheeling around a mother star. In Götze's neoclassical version, the condensed objects were not exactly what we understand today as planets, but rather the titular gods themselves.

This slender scientific heresy, expounded in the rapturous and instantly forgotten treatise *Der Sichtbar Olymp oder Himmel Aufgeklärt* (Visible Olympus, or Enlightened Heaven), was published at Leipzig in early 1799. It merits no more than a nod. Like Pandora's box, this book doesn't resist curiosity, but requires that the cover—at a glimpse of the contents—be immediately snapped shut to prevent them from escaping. Those were the years of the *incroyables*. Götze and his treatise are justly classed among the incredible events.

Formulated by Immanuel Kant in 1755, the nebular hypothesis, even the very word *nebula*, was much too suggestive to be forgotten. Which is to say that it was sufficiently nebulous to admit of almost any meaning. According to Götze, the originary nebula consisted entirely of Jove's will (*Zeus Wille*), a teleological power that nevertheless did not exclude whim, since instead of creating the universe he could have created something else altogether (obviously at Leipzig too, the transition from the century of light to the century of smoke had loosened the theological reins a bit). For us, the most pertinent whim occurred precisely when Jove's will started to turn, condense, become the sun, Mercury, etc., until among the objectified etc. we discover Jove himself, concretely and properly materialized in the largest and most majestic of the planets.

Here, to be fair to the author, we should quote his own words, because the guiding concept is much more imprecise and metaphysical than can be expressed in ours. But sad to say, Götze is a prolix writer, verbose and digressive, and no quotation of him on a given subject, no matter how brief, can be compressed into a few pages without serious reductiveness and, worse, betrayal. This is actually a genetic peculiarity of German thinkers. Condensing ruins them; so does transcription. The most one can do is to wander about them.

At the risk of illuminating and hence destroying Götze's ideas, we shall endeavor to describe a brief glimpse inside his box, possessed of the reassuring certainty that it will be shut at once and restored to its centuries-old rejection. The most striking aspect of this vision is the double nature attributed to the heavenly bodies. From the moment of condensation, they adopt their traditional names, nearly always in the Latin forms: Mercury, Venus, Mars, Jove, Saturn, and Uranus. The Sun, however, is called Helios, the moon Artemis, and the earth—perhaps through some unknown Teutonic affinity—Oops.

In addition to bearing the names of the Olympian deities (or some of them), the planets assume their familiar physical shapes.

Jove is a dignified patriarch, Venus a young woman, Mars a renowned soldier, and so forth. One must not suppose, in this Tiepolesque heaven, that the gods roam around naked. In fact, their gowns and togas emanate an intense glow—excepting only Mercury who, because of his nearness to Helios, cavorts in his birthday suit and hence often appears as a dark point. The most distinctive outfit belongs to Saturn: a series of rings. "It isn't matched," the author observes, "among any people on the earth. Nonetheless, it would be more becoming on a woman than a man." *Mann* writes Götze, with telling precision.

Helios is simply dressed in fire. All of these personages possess arms and legs and such like divine trifles. But they are in reality round, made of solid rock, and, like the earth, Oops, inhabited by myriad animals, plants, human beings, mountains, corvettes, clouds, varieties of filth, poultices, snow, and insects. Artemis alone is unpopulated, because being a virgin she has never been fertilized. The Sun composes lyrics and sings; the others, besides revolving around him, compose horoscopes and diligently attend to their specific duties, although not in their own spheres. This means that Mars can provoke wars anywhere but on Mars; this and only this planet is free from war. Similarly, Venus is devoid of desire, Mercury ignores efficiency, the natives of Saturn do not measure time, and those of the Sun have no acquaintance with art. The moon, however, is a wilderness of lechery. Oops is entrusted with the duty of ensuring universal justice. This also explains why it is impossible among us.

The idea that the planets are at once spiritual numen and material bodies was implicitly accepted by the ancients, or nearly all of them. Yet explicitly, on the scientific and practical level, which is the level of measurement, no ancient thinker of note ever affirmed or seriously thought that the intensity of Mars' radiance depended on the cuirass he might be wearing. Only

Götze, on the threshold of the nineteenth century, hazarded this cosmological hypothesis, in its pre-Romantic divagation. A man of the North, he didn't find it impossible to imagine a sphere of solid rock—on the one hand—subject to Newton's indisputable laws, sprouting eyes, arms, and legs from its shining rotundity, clad in a gown or toga, holding a lyre, scythe or hourglass, possessing hair, will, or feminine graces, and—on the other hand—a single, compact body swarming with human lice, themselves carriers of lice, grazed by mountains, cable cars, hot-air balloons, oceans (of ice on Saturn, fire on Helios).

Only Götze commanded the German coherence and, at this stage, the decidedly nineteenth-century precision to calculate in millions of tons the weight of Jove, father of the gods, his daughter Venus, and the most obese of his children, the Sun. His book contains an engraving by Hans von Aue which shows the huntress Artemis enclosed in her own crater-riddled globe. Another shows the originary nebula with seven spiral arms and the gods dragged by the whirlwind, all of them still babies.

Roger Babson

New Boston, in New Hampshire, was the first and only site of the Gravity Research Foundation, considered by its detractors to be the most useless scientific institute in the twentieth century. Its declared aim was the discovery of a substance capable of isolating and annulling the force of gravity.

Two famous men unwittingly contributed to launching the project. The first was H.G. Wells, whose novel *The First Men in the Moon* refers to the discovery of an alloy (called "cavorite" after its inventor) which achieves the above-mentioned aim. The second contributor was Thomas Alva Edison, a versatile inventor himself. One day, in conversation with his wealthy friend Roger Babson, Edison remarked: "Always remember, Babson, you don't know nothin' about nothin'. You've got to find something that isolates from gravity. I think it's coming about from some alloy." Babson was both a hard-bitten realist and a dreamy idealist, a combination that sometimes produces interesting results. He seems, in addition, to have been extremely ignorant.

The town of New Boston was chosen as the site of the Foundation for the sole reason that, although named after Boston, it was quite far from Boston in the event that Boston was destroyed by an atomic bomb. Babson's initial project was rather simple: testing alloys of every imaginable metal until he came across the one that caused the desired effect.

Since the possible alloys are virtually infinite, he soon realized the task would turn out to be infinite. Hence, the Foundation decided to busy itself with other, less monotonous activities which still hinged on gravitational problems. To take but one example: it organized a crusade against chairs, viewed as devices entirely unable to fend off the forces that gravity exerts on our bodies. According to Babson, these forces can be conquered simply by sitting on a carpet.

In 1949, the Foundation contacted two magazines, *Popular Mechanics* and *Popular Science*—both very popular indeed—and ran the following ad:

GRAVITY
If you are interested in gravity, write us.
No expense to you.

The ad was a failure. The Foundation then instituted a prize for the best essay on gravity. The text could not exceed 1500 words, and it had to address one of these topics: 1) how to obtain an alloy with the power to isolate, reflect, or absorb gravity; 2) how to obtain some substance, the atoms of which can be agitated or shuffled in the presence of gravity so as to produce heat without paying for it; and 3) some other reasonable method of turning a profit from the force of gravity. The first prize was one thousand dollars.

In 1951, the Foundation held its first International Conference—at New Boston, of course. The participants were invited to sit in special anti-gravitational chairs designed to facilitate blood circulation. To those who already suffered from circulatory problems the organizers offered tablets of Priscolene, a drug developed by Babson to combat gravity. In an adjoining hall Isaac Newton's bed was put on display. Babson had recently acquired it in England.

Kept alive by Babson, the Foundation generated publicity, not so much through the annual prize for the best essay against gravity, conferred by a jury of physics professors, as through a spate of moralizing scientific pamphlets which were regularly distributed to individuals and institutions interested in this field of research: libraries, universities, eminent scientists. The publications contained such observations as the following:

> Many thoughtful people believe that spiritual forces can modify the pull of gravity as illustrated by the story of certain Old Testament prophets having risen to the skies, and the Ascension of Jesus. The incident of Jesus walking on the water should not be ignored. People often ask why Angels are always shown defying gravity.

Mary Moore's essay on the theme of "Gravity and Posture" proposes the use of a close-fitting bodice or corset to "prevent gravity from pulling us too far forward or too far backward, which in so doing makes us old before our time." In the attack on chairs, written by Babson himself, the founder of the Foundation explains why sitting on carpets is more hygienic. If sitting in this fashion turns out to be impossible (because there is no carpet, or because the carpet is dirty), one can resort to the expedient of squatting. If this too is impossible, then a stool can be used, no higher than eight inches.

The worst effects of gravity occur when, through grave indifference, we sleep on our backs. To avoid falling into this pernicious habit, a rubber ball, two inches in diameter, may be buttoned into the collar of a nightshirt or pajamas. "This can best be accomplished," writes Babson, "by having a pocket [at the] back of the neck into which the ball would be kept during the night, and yet from which it could be removed when the night clothes go to the laundry." Everyone is free, however, to solve the tailoring problem in his or her own way.

Another essay by Babson, "Gravity and Ventilation," extols the wholesome practice of leaving every window open, at all times, summer and winter, whatever the weather. The author confesses to discovering the virtues of ventilation at a very young age. It was then that he fell seriously ill with tuberculosis, but, thanks to a method of his own invention (refusing to close doors and windows), he regained his health in a few months. Later, as an adult, Babson continued to work in an office exposed to the elements, whether snow or howling wind, wrapped in his battery-heated overcoat. On certain days, the room was so cold that his secretary, swathed entirely in blankets, was forced to hit the typewriter keys with rubber hammers in unison with the founder's dictation.

Babson discovered that the evacuation of bad air requires floors built on a slight incline and walls perforated with outlets so the force of gravity can drain away the stale air (as if it were so much dirty water). Such a house was constructed at New Boston: all the floors sloped half an inch to the foot.

Roger Babson, best known as a stock-market tipster, was also the owner of a diamond company, a huge firm that produced canned lobster, a factory that made fire alarms, a chain of super-markets, an office building in Boston, and much land and live-stock in New Mexico, Arizona, and Florida. Perhaps only one fear darkened his life: the atomic bomb. In another of his insti-tutions, Utopia College in Kansas, the buildings were all con-nected by underground tunnels as a precaution against a nuclear attack. For the same reason, Babson made one hundred identical deposits in one hundred different banks scattered across the en-tire United States, from Puerto Rico to Alaska to Hawaii.

Klaus Nachtknecht

For years after the discovery of radium in 1898, much attention was focused on its marvelous properties, especially the therapeutic ones. The information was vague and uncertain, but nonetheless widely circulated. Setting out from the optimistic premise that every discovery serves some useful purpose, which the available facts rarely denied (if one excepts the North and South Poles), the honest journalism of the period gave due importance to every sort of hypothesis concerning this new source of radiation, all of them utterly false. Just as the most fashionable in eighteenth-century society volunteered to endure electric shock for its sheer oddity, so the beautiful people at the start of twentieth century desired exposure to radioactivity to improve their health.

From Karlsbad to Ischia, thermal waters and mud baths were authoritatively analyzed and discovered to be radioactive in some measure—as everything in the universe is destined to be. Waters and mud baths were considered more precious, however, and their newly salubrious status was announced to the public through huge billboards and inserts in newspapers. In Budapest, Arthur Koestler's father, a soap manufacturer, performed analyses on soil from which he derived several ingredients. And revealing them to be radioactive, like all the soil on the earth, the elder Koestler sold his bars of radioactive soap with notable success, using the brand name "Radical." Not unexpectedly, their beneficial qualities made the skin increasingly more healthy and beautiful. Koestler's example was imitated in other countries. When the bomb exploded over Hiroshima, and many realized that radioactivity didn't always result in a splendid complexion, the soap underwent a change in name and advertising. With lucrative obstinacy, however, hot springs and mud baths proclaimed their appeal to the secret forces of nature for years to come.

In 1922, an amazing orogenic venture was launched in the same spirit of science and publicity: the chain of volcanic hotels run by Nachtknecht and Pons. Sebastián Pons was the son of a Valparaíso-based hotelier who owned a famous chain of typical seaside accommodations. The international press frequently recalled the Asiatic luxury of the Gran Pons at Viña del Mar on the Pacific, as well as the European squalor of the Nuevo Pons at Mar del Plata on the Atlantic. Yet Sebastián had the good fortune to meet a German émigré geologist of no fame whatsoever, called Klaus Nachtknecht.

Pinched by the difficulties of a shaky exile, Nachtknecht earned his living as a professor of German, an elective in the Faculty of Sciences. This setting obviously inflamed his insatiable geological passion, which took a dark turn with the mute, multitudinous, and overwhelming nearness of the Andes. While his compatriots died at Ypres like flies in a skillet, Nachtknecht, in the greenhouse of his impenetrable language, cultivated diverse theories in monastic silence. To Pons, who was his chosen disciple—in fact, his only disciple—he revealed his dearest, most dreamy, and most original theories concerning volcanic radiation.

In brief, Nachtknecht discovered that magma emitted radiation possessed with an enormous vivifying potency, so that nothing was more conducive to health than living on a volcano—or rather underneath it. For confirmation he cited the beauty and longevity of the Neapolitans, the intelligence of the Hawaiians, the physical resistance of the Icelanders, the fertility of the Indonesians. Displaying a typically German wittiness, he concocted an up-to-date graph that plotted the length of the male member in various peoples and countries around the world. And without fail the enviable qualities and sizes were located in the most volcanically active regions. This graph, which in academic spheres might have been greeted with perplexity, if anything, wound up convincing his young pupil.

Having inherited his father's hotels in 1919 and his aunt's molybdenum mine in 1920, Pons entrusted his beach holdings to an English administrator (hence trustworthy) and his mines to a legless Chilean engineer (hence even more trustworthy). Thereafter, with his friend and professor, he hurled himself into a project that made him famous at first but in the end so poor that he was forced to accept the post of Chilean consul to Colón (in Panama), a starving wage in a hellish climate.

It was Nachtknecht who first advanced the idea of a spa on the side of a volcano. Of course, the guests need not be actually sick (besides, who isn't?). People of any age and physical condition were welcome. Indeed, the more healthy and vigorous the clients, the more secure the establishment's reputation as a health resort.

The Maestro was loath to publish books in a language that seemed to him devoid of logic—like Spanish (a language that for centuries refused the greatest ornament of thought and persists, as is known, in concluding every sentence with a verb). Yet Pons induced him to prepare at least a few pamphlets, not simply to generate publicity, but to spread the principles and merits of the new radiation among the unknowing public.

Thus appeared *El Magma Saludable* (The Salubrious Magma) near the end of 1920 and in 1921 both *Acerquémonos al Volcán*

(Approach to the Volcano) and *Lava y Gimnasia* (Lava and Gymnastics). Pons translated all three texts from German, or at least corrected the translations, which were published at Santiago in a practically unlimited edition on paper of such poor quality that the only truly legible pages were those printed on one side. Two years later, contemporary with the construction of the first hotel in the chain, another publication appeared under Nachtknecht's signature, *Rayos de Vida* (Rays of Life, 33 pages).

Pons's original plan consisted of four luxury spas, or clinic-hotels, built on the sides of Kilauea in Hawai'i, Etna in Sicily, Pillén Chillay in what was then the territory of Neuquén in Argentina, and Cosigüina in Nicaragua. He also anticipated a fifth inn for recluses in a place still to be determined on the island of Tristan da Cunha in the Atlantic (or possibly the adjacent island, justly called Inaccessible).

From 1916 onward the Hawaiian project encountered insurmountable difficulties from the federal authorities at Volcanoes National Park. In 1922, Pons's agents acquired a parcel of land on Etna at an altitude of approximately two thousand meters. But a few months later it was engulfed by a sea of lava and effectively vanished from the land registry, becoming yet another crater in this eternally voracious volcano.

In Nicaragua, the agent at Managua inexplicably prolonged the arrangements. It was later learned that he had been imprisoned on a political charge and was performing the land transfer from prison. Inevitably he was not permitted to acquire mountains near the Honduran border. Out of the blue he communicated that Cosigüina had shown no signs of life since remote 1835 (this too proved false), and so he offered a more suitable tract on the blooming island of Omotepe, in Lake Nicaragua, exactly midway between two giant volcanoes, Madera and Concepción, both highly active and lush with vegetation.

Pons contacted the Nicaraguan embassy to learn more. He tracked down the cultural attaché, who explained that the land in question was actually the site of a huge penitentiary on Omotepe, and most likely the agent was trying to sell him the prison where he was doing time for his political errors. Thus, the mining hotelier was forced to abandon his Nicaraguan project as well.

His only alternative was to focus his attention on the two southern projects that remained, one Patagonian, the other Atlantic. For the first he would have to deal with the Argentines, for the second with the English: both were trustworthy, European, and usefully stingy and stern. Pons imagined that Tristan da Cunha could be easily reached by sea, which seemed plausible enough since it was an island. He subsequently discovered that the regular service boats arrived only once a year, at the end of October. The boats, moreover, departed from Sant'Elena, the site of the governor's permanent residence. But no one in Valparaíso knew how to reach Sant'Elena. And no one had ever attempted it. This guaranteed not only that the clients' stay would be lengthy, but that the construction of the hotel would be problematic. In addition, the volcanoes on the island had for centuries maintained their dignified dormancy intact.

Hence, Pons decided to postpone his voyage to Tristan da Cunha and concentrate all his efforts on Neuquén. Pillén Chillay rose, and still rises, on the border between Neuquén and Río Negro, and it was easily accessible from San Carlos de Bariloche. The road, covered with sharp rocks, was most panoramic, although the locals—four in all—called it wheel-shattering. These four people were stubbornly Germanic. They reigned solitary over wilderness inhabited by thousands of sheep whose long wool touched the earth. They also possessed an equally immense number of pigs.

Amidst sheep and pigs Pons quickly discovered that any type

of communication was impossible with the Germans who were, furthermore, pig-headed in their insistence that their country won the World War. The available vehicles—a broken down Model T Ford and a sturdier but smashed Studebaker—forced Pons to head for Bariloche on foot because the knowing horses refused to travel on the rock-strewn road.

At Bariloche the locals were all Germans too, and they exhibited a remarkable suspicion toward the Chileans, who were traditionally considered bandits or whores, depending on their sex. Sebastián finally managed to dispatch a telegram to Nachtknecht, who had remained in Santiago. To this summons the Maestro responded at once: he took the Transandean train, reached Puente del Inca and stayed there a month and a half, blocked by the snow. From Puente del Inca Nachtknecht eventually went south to Mendoza, via Uspallata. Four months later he arrived at Bariloche.

At the professor's arrival, the entire German community shook off their Patagonian lethargy, and in a very brief time the hotel at Pillén Chillay became a reality. It seemed as if every hill, craggy peak, ancient cedar, and erratic boulder hid a German, ready to work as gardener, barman, waitress, chauffeur, or woodcutter—even on a volcano. Many of them were Austrians and Poles, but they were called Germans generically, just as "Turks" was the generic name given to the numerous Arabs in the vicinity. In time, they too flocked to offer Nachtknecht their not less erratic services.

The volcano was rather beautiful, what with the snow at the top, the slopes blanketed with forests, and, down below, two lakes in the unusual shape of parentheses, deep blue and icy cold. The hotel, constructed with wood and masonry, rose halfway up the mountainside at a point that was fairly well heated. Snowstorms rendered it inaccessible only five months a year.

Klaus Nachtknecht

Besides typical icy baths with Finnish saunas and ski trails with steam-driven cable cars, the services were to include a vast range of properly volcanic activities: baths in hot lava, sulfuric inhalations, caustic swimming pools, gymnastics during tremors, telluric games of various kinds, radioactive grottoes, boulder avalanches caused by nitroglycerine explosions daily at noon, sulfurous air conditioning in the guest rooms and the great dining hall, nudist hikes to the craters and nearby fissures, dealers of volcanic stone worked in the native style, and a splendid seismograph in the ballroom. There was also a plan to build a volcanic theater, Italian-style, for evening performances and fireworks in the snow, and even some pig-breeding near the double lake, purely for the naturalists.

These last few plans remained, however, at the planning stage. In fact, two months before the inaugural ceremony, on the occasion of a most inauspicious eruption in March 1924, the entire hotel disappeared beneath a layer—six meters thick—of volcanic detritus, dust, ash, stone, and lava. Nachtknecht was buried, together with most of the employees on the site. Pons was luckier: he happened to be in Bariloche. He needed to sell everything he owned to pay damages to the victims' families, seventy-five dead and two burnt.

Absalon Amet

Absalon Amet, clockmaker of La Rochelle, can certainly be dubbed the secret precursor of a not insignificant area in early modern philosophy—perhaps even the precursor of *all* modern philosophy. He was, more precisely, a pioneer in that vast field of inquiry motivated by a voluptuary and decorative aim: the random combination of words that are rarely combined in current usage, with the subsequent deduction of any meaning or meanings that might eventually be extracted from the whole. For example: "History is the movement of nothingness toward time," "History is the movement of time toward nothingness," "The flute is dialectic," and similar combinations. A man of the Eighteenth Century, a man of wit, Amet never pretended to satire or knowledge; a man of mechanisms, he had no other wish but to exhibit a mechanism. Therein lay hidden and threatening, although unknown to him, a future teeming with horrid professors of semiotics and brilliant avant-garde poets.

Amet invented and constructed a Universal Philosophy, which in the beginning occupied a good portion of a table, but in the end filled an entire room. Essentially, the apparatus consisted of a rather simple assemblage of cogwheels, which were spring-driven and regulated in their movement by a special gear that periodically stopped the mechanism. In the initial version, five cogwheels of different diameters were coaxial with as many cylinders, large and small, covered completely with little plates which were each imprinted with a word. These plates rotated behind a wooden screen provided with narrow rectangular windows, so that if one stood in front of the screen, every rotation allowed a sequence of words to be read, always random but not always devoid of sense. Marie Plaisance Amet, the clockmaker's only child, read these phrases and transcribed the most curious and apodictic in a huge ledger.

The words on the first cylinder were all substantives—in French, of course—and each was preceded by the corresponding article. The second cylinder carried verbs. The third prepositions, idiomatic and unidiomatic. The fourth bore adjectives, and the fifth more substantives, although a different selection from the first. The cylinders could be spun back and forth at will, a feature that yielded an almost infinite variety of combinations. Nonetheless, this first version of the Universal Philosophy, *à six mots* (six-worded), was clearly much too rudimentary, since it could only furnish sentences of the following type: "Life-gravitates-toward-the-same-point," "A woman-chooses-under-low-thrusts," "The-universe-emerges-from-much-passion," and other thoughts even more inane.

For a humble mechanician like Amet, concocting a Philosophy that was more developed—capable of producing, in other words, more daring syntactic turns and more memorable sentences—was only a question of patience and time, two qualities that the emaciated Protestant community of La Rochelle did not deny its members. He added adverbs of every sort: manner, place, time, quantity, quality. He added conjunctions, negatives, substantive verbs, and a hundred like refinements. As the clockmaker attached more wheels and cylinders and cut more narrow windows in the wooden screen, the Philosophy augmented in volume, but also in surface. In the young Marie Plaisance the noise of the mechanism evoked the internal rumble of a bustling brain, while in the light of one, two, and finally three candles every rotation offered a thought, every combination a theme for reflection on the long autumnal evenings before the gray sea.

In her ledger, she did not simply make note of such sentences as "The cat is indispensable to the progress of religion," or "To wed tomorrow is not worth an egg now." No, her pen also recorded, without her awareness, countless concepts that were then obscure, but which a century, two centuries later would be considered penetrating. For example, in *Pensées et Mots Choisis du Philosophe Mécanique Universel* (Select Thoughts and Words from the Universal Mechanical Philosophy), the collection published at Nantes in 1774 under the names of Absalon and Plaisance Amet, we find a sentence from Lautréamont ("The fish you feed swear no fraternity"), one from Rimbaud ("The sapient music lacks our desire"), and another from Laforgue ("The sun lays aside the papal stole"). What sense of future irreality induced the young lady—or her father on her behalf—to choose from thousands of sentences precisely those that would one day merit the anthology?

But perhaps the most remarkable are the sentences that possess a character purely philosophical, in the broadest sense of the word. How surprising to read the following in a book from 1774: "The real is rational"; "Boiled meat is life, broiled meat death"; "Art is sentiment"; "History is bunk"; "Existence is being toward death"; "Hell is everybody else"; "The text is always already deconstructed"; and many other combinations that have today become more or less renowned.

Still, it is not surprising to learn that three copies of the

Amets' book were recently found in the small, disorganized public library of Pornic in the lower Loire valley. The discovery may appear belated at this juncture: the day will soon arrive—if in fact it isn't already here—when every proposition in the Universal Mechanical Philosophy is welcomed with due respect into the generous bosom of the History of Western Philosophy.

Carlo Olgiati

In 1931, on the threshold of his eightieth birthday, Carlo Olgiati of Abbiategrasso finally issued his fundamental work in three volumes, *Il metabolismo storico* (Historical Metabolism), the sole publication of the "La Redentina" press at Novara, which was mainly a sweets factory owned by the author.

This notable example of the lively Lombard intellect, today virtually extinct, endured a miserable life, which is to say not much life at all. Immediately confiscated by the Fascist authorities, it did not enjoy a better fate in subsequent years, so that only a dozen copies of the entire edition are extant, nearly all incomplete and in private hands. In 1956, one of the complete copies was discovered in the tidy stacks of the Duke University library. And in 1958 this copy, precious as an incunabulum, became the basis of a shortened Photostat edition, the only accessible source of the intermittent tremors of attention still provoked by Olgiati's name decades after his death.

The Maestro devoted more than twenty years to the elaboration of his biological socioeconomic theory. A first version, senescent but far from exhaustive, was entitled *La lotta dei gruppi nella fauna e nella flora* (The Group Struggle Among Fauna and Flora). It was published in 1917, at the height of the war, and met with even less success than the definitive version would later encounter. The author himself withdrew it from all the libraries of Milan, Novara, Alessandria, and Casal Monferrato, perhaps displeased with its incompleteness, perhaps irritated by the fact that no newspaper, magazine, or publication of any kind ran a single review of it.

The last among the great constructors of systems, Olgiati was also famous as the proprietor of a bakery for biscotti called "Prussians," a local specialty of Cuggiono near Abbiategrasso. For reasons entirely foreign to philosophy, he was forced to shut down the bakery—on the bank of the River Ticino, but on the brink of failure—a year after Italy's entrance into the war. The establishment succeeded in reopening its doors in 1919. The biscotti, although the same as before, were now sold under the more agreeable name of "Redentini," Little Deliverers. In the interval, Olgiati slightly modified his conception of history. To this more coherent vision he would devote the long years of relative peace and unquestioned poverty that followed.

Intelligently inserted into the most popular trends of modern thought, his is a biochemical philosophy of history linked to a precise, complex, and improbable genetic-economic theory. Every aspect of historical becoming is viewed as the emanation and result of the inevitable conflict between the various groups that distinguish a population, whether animal or vegetable. This conflict, irreconcilable and ubiquitous, he called the "group struggle" and defined as the prime mover of historical metabolism.

The chief groups (O, A, B, AB) were discovered in 1900 by Landsteiner. Olgiati lacked the opportunity to take into account the MN and the RH, discovered in more recent times, because he had already died. These other groups, however, presented no particular problems with regard to the effusions from one group to another, the principal cause of the above-mentioned permanent conflict.

Carlo Olgiati

Under the name of Olgiatism or—for a brief time—historical metabolism, the theory both hypothesizes and demonstrates
the inevitability of Olgiatism, understood as an ideal state wherein all groups merge into a single group, so that concepts of the
State, law, money, hunting, sex, police, wages, and the transformation of energy into heat and mechanical labor no longer perform any function and, so to speak, vanish from history.

Given the incompatibility that exists between diverse groups,
an individual from group O may not receive fluids from any
other group. In contrast, his (or her) fluids are quite acceptable
in all four groups, and therefore O is usually given the title of
universal donor. Members of group A or B can only receive
fluids from their own type, excepting those from O. Members of
AB, however, accept fluids from every other group. This holds
true, according to the author, for the fauna and flora of the earth
in toto.

As early as his first publication in '17, Olgiati hazarded a definition of history as the interaction—or "struggle," in the words of
the title—between various groups. The scientific knowledge in
this field was rather vague at the time; Carlo Olgiati's knowledge
was even more vague. Further progress in his research and new
contacts with interesting tourist and medical publications in
Bellinzona and Mendrisio led the philosopher to formulate a
much more general and comprehensive theory, which he later
called historical metabolism. From the very beginning, the adherents of this theory were called Olgiatists.

Basically, the Olgiatists believed that history—otherwise
called social meteorology—was governed by biochemical laws
that the human mind (read: Olgiati) should be in a position to
discover, whether through direct observation of historical meteorological facts or through laboratory research. The knowledge of
these laws enables the theorist to foresee the future developments

of the social atmospheric climate, down to the smallest details. The most enthusiastic Olgiatists, like Romp from Vallebruna (in open disagreement with the notorious Vittorio Volini), did not hesitate to discuss the "granite foundations of objective meteorological necessity" whereon rests Olgiatic determinism (also called Olgiatian and Olgiastic). As often happens, even the Maestro's doubts became dogma to his students.

The theory foresees, indeed postulates, the inevitable final victory of the universal donors, or group O. Paradoxically, this certainty ensured that the most assiduous Olgiatists would be recruited from members of the other groups. Since the victory of the universal donors was in fact inevitable, it was unclear why they needed to strive, toil, and suffer to bring about an event that must in any case happen. As for the motives that drive A and B to marry another's cause with such deep commitment, various hypotheses were advanced by the Torinese psychiatric school, none entirely satisfying. The Roman branch maintained that it was a matter of anality pure and simple, a tendency to exhibit and stick out the anus for a comical and pedagogical end. In B, the anality very frequently becomes oral.

A few words can hardly suffice to summarize the great Olgiatian conceptual edifice contained in the three dense volumes of the classic '31 text. The best approach is to begin with the laws that regulate the historical meteorological course of living matter. The first law determines its direction. In its most general form, this law affirms that any modification in the oxidation rate sets going necessary modifications in every sector of fauna and flora. Ideas, number of legs, judicial system, the search for food, even religious belief and the shape of the horn constitute integral parts of the phytozoological superstructure, and they are inevitably compelled to change according to changes in the metabolic oxidizing process. This process directs the transformation of chemical energy from glycids, lipids, proteides, and nucleoproteides into heat and mechanical labor. Since technological development leads ineluctably to always larger organs of reproduction, the moment will arrive when only the community of viruses and plankton will be able to furnish adequate support for the constantly augmenting production of heat and mechanical labor.

It would seem incorrect to assert, writes Olgiati, that ideas and other nervous and anatomical factors have no influence on social meteorology. It is important to recognize, however, that they are not independent agents. Nor can it be argued that historical degradation is controlled exclusively by material or chemical forces. Still, it must be admitted that various organic factors commonly called idealist—like athletic competition, the concept of property, extrafamilial incest, and the prohibition against eating raw human flesh—are themselves the product of the social oxidation process and its direct and indirect impact on fauna and flora.

It has been objected (especially by a critical progressive faction nostalgic for the Enlightenment, at once reactionary and independent) that if the broad range of metabolic processes always allows for the possibility of determining the cause of nearly every natural historical meteorological development, one cannot deny that many factors in the oxidizing exchange are the effect—to the extent that they are causative—of developments that are either latent or present in the biochemical economy. For example, changes in women's fashion, transformations in the sexual customs of the religious, in table manners, even in the names of newspapers exercise a calculable influence on the consumption of glycids, lipids, proteids, and nucleoproteids and hence become factors determining the production of heat and mechanical labor. The outcome is a true labyrinth of causes and effects in which any prediction would appear to be impossible.

Very sensibly Olgiati refutes this objection by postulating that any fundamental change in phytozoological metabolism possesses a character that is not so much ideological as technological. Technological progress, although dependent on diverse developments (political, athletic, astronomical, epidemical, among others), is unstoppable. Hence, both fauna and flora will always tend to produce increasing quantities of heat and mechanical work. It is more generally agreed that the chemical interpretation of history is a bit over the top in denying any autonomy whatsoever to the intellectual and spiritual development of viruses and phytoplankton. Nevertheless, it must be granted that Olgiati immensely enriched the panorama of the zoobotanical sciences (including ethology and ecology) by compelling their recognition that the sheer growth and multiplication of biochemical, technological, and energetic transformations underlie important evolutionary aspects in animals and vegetables—especially as producers and reproducers of mechanical labor.

In the dialectical process of material metabolism, one can distinguish two opposing yet fundamental moments, which occur alternately in succession and in superimposition. The first, synthetic moment is called anabolic: it forms the substance that is unique and specific to every single organism or phytozoological organ, and it stores reserve material, always at the expense of substances that fauna and flora derive from the external environment in order to grow, maintain themselves, and repair continual wear and tear. The second moment, the analytic, is called catabolic: it is characterized by the decomposition of reserve material and exchange products into their simplest constituents, the residue of which is usually eliminated through so-called institutions of excretion (toilets, insane asylums, cemeteries, zoos, rubbish dumps, hospitals, prisons, crematoria, and such like).

For Olgiati, every truly important advance in energy issues from the total dialectical conflict between these two moments or principles. It follows that any precaution which relaxes the tension among fauna and flora prematurely or, in more precise terms, any oxidation that is not total and instantaneous is considered an obstacle to the progress of the phytozoologic organism as a whole. The absolute necessity of revolution follows from the negation of progressive value in partial oxidations and, generally, in any precaution that is meteorologically interlocutory in character (i.e., involves a fluid conversation).

Here it won't be superfluous to observe that the thinker of Abbiategrasso was not, as the saying goes, a person of dialectically mature years. Hence, his theory presents many lacunae, if not simply holes. At the very least, one must acknowledge that the dialectical process itself, as he describes it, requires that every revolution be followed (if the aim is to prolong the life of history, animal and vegetable alike) by a second revolution, then another, and another, ad infinitum, until complete catabolism occurs. In fact, confronted with this objection, the surviving Olgiatists tend to take refuge in the so-called "mysticism of groups." In light of later discoveries, however, this notion also appears devoid of heuristic value, at least in postulating a causal relation with viral and phytoplankton metabolism.

Olgiati assigned special importance to the now indisputable truth that at times various groups experience internal conflicts. These conflicts are manifested not only at the moment of transfusion, with often lethal results, but also in the flow of everyday life (as when clashing articles of clothing are chosen), with not less lethal results. All the same, he wanted to radicalize the terms of this natural chemical antagonism, going so far as to assert that various groups do not possess common oxidizing processes, nor can they ever, and their struggle (which figures in the title to his debatable dissertation of '17) will end only with the final and total victory of the universal donors. Whereupon all the other groups will be definitively relegated to the institutions of excretion.

His apocalyptic conviction is linked to his blind faith (characteristic of northern Italy) in the transcendent superiority of private over mental activity, even if done in the open. In Olgiatian thought, the group struggle is clearly identified with the immanent conflict between movement and paralysis. As Heisenberg's principle decrees, the conflict is perforce a conflict to the last drop, and it doesn't admit of any truce or settlement. The victory of group O will not be complete without the extinction of every other group, A, B, and especially AB. Thus it seems inevitable that before achieving the ultimate orgasm, the conflictual peristalsis must flow into the so-called "dictatorship of group O" as a transitory meteorological form of excretion during the movement from the anabolic to the catabolic order.

With regard to the highly controversial transformation of historical atmospheric energy into heat and mechanical labor, the rare third volume of Olgiati's *Metabolism* elaborates a theory that is particularly attractive, but not equally convincing. It is based partly on the principles of the English zoologist Abel Roberto—which in that period were repudiated everywhere in the civilized world except the Lombard enclave—and partly on Olgiati's own conception of ecological surplus value or economization, defined here as the difference between basal and additional metabolism. Additional metabolism varies in proportion to the expenditure of energy needed for mental work, the regulation of moisture, digestive processes, and secondary and tertiary activities, such as distribution and services. Basal metabolism, in contrast, corresponds to the lowest, irreducible expenditure of energy in the phytozoological complex—in other words, to the level of the global oxidizing process of all fauna and flora in basal conditions (complete privation, abstention from any pleasures of the senses, total immobility, total absence of thought, pleasant background music).

The rate of basal metabolism, according to Olgiati, is taken directly from the universal donors of group O (including viruses and phytoplankton), which the author occasionally designates with a generic, archaizing name: "the proletariat of nature." In such conditions of sub-existence or alienation, the energetic expenditure for survival is determined by the oxidizing processes necessary to maintain cardiac, respiratory, renal, and liver function, muscle tone, the digestive tract, and the endocrine glands. The author implies that the ideal state, which he derived from measuring this minimum or proletarian metabolism, absolutely excludes the exercise of the reproductive function, which by definition is reserved for fauna and flora at a high level of oxidation.

Now it is quite evident, even in the eyes of a Milanese, that in minimum basal conditions the proletariat not only survive but in some way reproduce, despite huge biochemical difficulties. The author sidesteps this contradiction by revealing that the level necessary for reproduction is calculated as a fraction of the difference between additional and basal metabolism, previously defined as ecological surplus value or economization. Since group O is theoretically precluded from this ecological economy and fated by the existing arrangement of fauna and flora to serve and be used exclusively by the other groups, especially AB, the reproductive level of viruses and phytoplankton is counted among the non-labor sources of income: namely, profit, rent, and interest.

The third volume of *Metabolism* is devoted in good part to theorizing the ecological exploitation of the universal donors by the other non-donor groups. And it is here that the most conspicuous aporias have been discovered. More serious still, the very dogma concerning the movement from anabolism to catabolism as the ineluctable condition of renewal was brilliantly refuted by the Englishman F.H. Lamie (see "Olgiati's End of Time," *Proceedings of the Aristotelian Society*, LXIII: 25–48). Lamie managed to demonstrate—in the laboratory, no less—that given the impossibility of returning from a generalized state of catabolism to a constructive state of anabolism, the only alternative that remains (and not only to viruses and phytoplankton) lies between death and an eternal catabolism, feeble and precarious, characterized by the progressive paralysis of every function, whether productive or reproductive. This would be tantamount, as Lamie so well explains, to proposing "an infinite comatose state as the supreme goal of life." The proposal seems unacceptable for fauna as well as flora.

Antoine Amédée Bélouin

In 1897 Antoine Amédée Bélouin unveiled Project Bélouin, destined to bring confusion to mass transit at the dawn of the twentieth century. Project Bélouin anticipated a new, ubiquitous network of underwater transport. Essentially, ingeniously, it meant a submarine train. Not unexpectedly, its aim encompassed little more than increasing beyond measure the wealth and glory of France, broker and bawd between incompatible oceans and seas, laureate builder of canals.

The inverse of a canal is in fact a tunnel, like the chunnel that currently joins France and England (despite financial troubles). Much more economically, Bélouin imagined two rails riveted to the sea floor and a train running, no, sliding or sailing over them. It would be an express, of course, which would not even stop to replenish the water supply. Performing the latter operation at the bottom of the sea, even in the practical eyes of the enthusiastic entrepreneur, seemed paradoxically problematic.

No site was more suitable to such a rapid transportation network than the Baltic—except that the Baltic didn't yet belong (or no longer belonged?) to France, even if powerful dynasties on its shores carried the names of Bernadotte and, albeit briefly, Valois. Bélouin presumed, however, that the prestige of the French government would easily enable him to obtain a right of preemption and protection for the useless floor of that sea, which, moreover, was ugly, foggy, cold, and in a certain sense still to be colonized.

One submarine railway from St. Petersburg to Kiel, another from Danzig to Stockholm, and the cross of Lorraine would be created, reconfirming the too often confirmed capacity for expansion that distinguishes the French genius. Yet this was the long-term goal of the project. As for the immediate future, various routes would henceforth be imposed with the chrism of inevitability: Calais–Dover, Le Havre–Southampton, and the Mediterranean triangle of Marseilles–Barcelona–Algiers–Genova, in addition to an eventual line for pleasure and big-game hunting, the Bastia–Civitavecchia. (See Antoine Amédée Bélouin, *Réseau Bélouin: Premier Projet de Chemin de Fer sous la Mer*, Limoges, 1897.)

In this manual for submerged railways, Bélouin admits—with as much generosity as frankness—his total technical and scientific incompetence in the diverse problems raised by his project. (In point of fact, he was a professor of Latin and Greek at a provincial *lycée*.) Yet he doesn't doubt that if entrusted to experts, the majority of these problems will be solved by themselves, so to speak. "The progress of modern science," he asserts,

> has been so dizzying in recent years that if, on the one hand, there no longer exists a Cicero who can sum up the entire body of knowledge, then on the other hand it could be said that the time is not far away when, thanks to the combined efforts of today's valiant scientists (*preux savants*), every human problem past and present will be solved, a development that will permit us more easily to pose, expose, and compose the problems of the future.

The reference to Cicero in this context serves only to evince

the author's originality. Little inclined to the technical fastidious-
ness of his contemporary, the fabulist Jules Verne, Bélouin prudently delegates to experts the task of resolving these issues
(among so many others): the thickness of the steel-plated sides of
the watertight coaches, which must withstand intense underwater pressure; the internal air pressure in the same coaches; the
efficient functioning of a steam locomotive on the sea floor;
lighting (with the means available in 1897); the laying of track in
the primordial mud; demolition works, bridge construction over
unfathomed depths, and similar operations; the precipitous
slopes of coastlines; the movement of vehicles from land to sea
and vice versa; danger signals; rescue procedures in case of minor
or major incidents; the resistance of water to motion; currents;
emergencies of a technical nature, such as the depletion of coal
supplies; communication between the coaches, and so forth.

To compensate for these omissions, Bélouin minutely describes the seats, cabins, and double-paned windows in the
coaches, which will be constructed in the shape of mortar shells
for reasons that have more to do with ballistics than hydrody-
namics. He describes the police force that will safeguard public
decency, both inside the train and at the customs checkpoints for
departures and arrivals; the heating system, a latticework grate
filled with anthracite pellets lit at the moment of departure; the
collision-proof shield of the locomotive, which will take the
form of a shark or, better, a swordfish (*narval*). He foresees one
armored carriage, perforated on each side with a row of gun por-
tals, to transport precious objects, gold ingots, and state docu-
ments. He foresees special compartments to transport corpses as
well as the clergy. And in conclusion he foresees, as an indirect
consequence of these cosmopolitan submarine contacts, a greater
fraternity among nations, although beneath the luminous and
inexhaustible sign of French ingenuity.

Armando Aprile

Armando Aprile possessed the consistency of a ghost. He left nothing behind, except for a name that sounds fake and an address that didn't belong to him. Both were printed on a poster that appeared one day in the streets of Rome. Ephemeral utopian, he proposed an order to the world, but the world seems not to have wanted it. The poster read as follows:

ATTENTION!!!
A VERY IMPORTANT MESSAGE

☞ LAUNCH DATE: 1/12/1968 ☜

I swear I shall enforce the following laws, if and when the world population joins me in displaying certain identifying signs, such as wearing their watches on their right wrists or affixing the initials "AA" to a visible part of their persons or clothing. We shall adopt green handkerchiefs, uniforms in a uniform color, white or blue, and black shoes, in case of mourning. Our flag will be white and/or blue.

These laws aim to establish an equality among six ward divisions. The First Ward is reserved for the first 36 Managers of the

World. Second Ward: the next 36,000 Managers of the World. Third Ward: Judges. Fourth Ward: Scientists, Doctors, Commissioners, Engineers, Lawyers, Generals, as well as officers and administrators of various sorts, including brigadiers in the Carabinieri, theater directors and producers, and coaches and trainers. Fifth Ward: Treasury, Admiralty, Carabinieri, Police, Students, Military, Clerical Workers, and so forth. Sixth Ward: Children, from birth to twelve years of age, and Prisoners convicted of homicide. The capital criminals will work ten hours a day; the other convicts will be paid wages and hence will work free for eight hours a day, until they finish paying for their crimes. Any of them can take advantage of our good conduct policy. Those who are released will work no more than five hours a day.

4. The unemployed will receive a daily wage as if they worked.

5. Retirees, whether because of age, accident, or illness, will receive a daily wage as when they worked, in addition to hospitalization, medicine, and housing—*gratis.*

6. Every youth regardless of height and sex may carry the flag, unless they have been convicted of homicide.

7. Wherever possible, every workplace will be air conditioned, fitted with the latest furnishings, maintained in maximum cleanliness, and so forth.

8. Whenever any citizen reaches twenty-one years of age, they will have the right to a new lodging, free of charge, in the town where their profession permits them to be resident.

9. We shall speak a single language. Dialect will be fined.

10. My new regulations for automobiles and other motor vehicles will allow us to avoid 90 percent of all accidents.

11. Taxation will cease, since everybody will be a dependent of World Management.

12. Deserts will be inhabited and cultivated. (My simple plan

will allow us to avoid disagreements between the North and South of every Nation.)

13. Divorce is permitted. Hence, it is better simply to avoid marriage.

14. As soon as possible I shall cause volcanoes to be extinguished since, apart from their sheer danger, they burn such an expanse of subsoil as to prove useless to our evolution today and perhaps tomorrow.

15. It is most likely that I shall succeed in removing the water from the seas and leaving only what is necessary for irrigation, since they pose a great danger to the planet Earth. What if someone immersed gigantic blenders in the seas? We would all die in a wink.

16. I promise immortality with a 90 percent success rate—i.e., youth can remain young, and the aged can regain their youth.

17. Whoever agrees with these laws should assist me financially in whatever way they can by sending a donation to this address:

> Aprile Armando
> c/o Giglio
> 243 St. Nicholas Ave.
> Brooklyn, New York 11237

Help me spread this message in every possible language throughout the World, while hindering the false laws that our enemies spread in their turn.

18. My identifying signs are: 1.54 meters tall, shoeless and hatless, thin build, dark-haired, florid complexion, scar on the right side of the thorax, a small wart near the right ear, face divided in half by a natural, nearly invisible line, surname and first name: Aprile Armando, born 29/12/1940.

Franz Piet Vredjuik

The nature of light was subject to a lengthy and disputatious postmortem between Christiaan Huygens and Isaac Newton, who were joined by bishops, lunatics, pharmacists, a prince of Thurn und Taxis, an entomologist from Concord, Massachusetts, and Goethe, among many others. Although their academic credentials were not always what the topic required, none presented fewer than Franz Piet Vredjuik, a gravedigger at Udenhout in the Low Countries—if his own testimony is true. He read only two books in his entire life: the Bible and the complete works of Linnæus. His boast rendered him unique in the fragmented field of post-Newtonian philosophy. It is stated explicitly (whether with arrogance or modesty remains unclear) in the preface to the only study he left us: *Universal Sin, or A Discourse on the Identity between Sound and Light* (Utrecht, 1776). As the reader may gather from the title, the purpose of this brief treatise is to demonstrate—or in fact to assert without any more demonstration than a series of precise appeals to intuition—that sound is light, degenerate light.

From a purely structural point of view, even if we admit what was then called the wave hypothesis, Vredjuik's proposal may appear tenable. Much less convincing, however, seems his justification: that the efficient and universal cause for the recurrent decline of light into sound is original sin.

To start with, the thesis presupposes a hierarchical relation between sound and light, which is so evident as not to merit any explanation: light is by definition much more noble than sound. This tacit prerogative still obtains today—when, that is, it doesn't provoke exasperation. Virtually nobody has read Vredjuik, but everybody agrees in recognizing the privileges of light. Nothing, for example, can surpass its speed. If it weren't for light, there'd be nothing else in the universe. Only light manages to do without matter. At the same time, however, nobody now maintains, like Vredjuik, that light possesses these qualities because it alone, amongst all the manifestations in the cosmos, has not undergone the consequences of Adam's sin. At the slightest touch of sin, light breaks down, becoming heat, filth, brutishness, noise.

The idea of a fundamental identity between light and sound flashed through Vredjuik's mind, he explains, just a few days after the arrival of his second-born, Margarethe. One night, about two in the morning, his daughter was bent on screaming, as Dutch infants are wont to do at that hour, when suddenly her screams reached an intense diapason so unusual that the father, his covers pulled tight around his ears, saw three stars spark like lightning in the pitch darkness. This was the first example of sound becoming light. Subsequent reflection led Vredjuik to conjecture a direct relation between this phenomenon and the fact that Margarethe had been baptized that very day. Since the baby hadn't yet committed any sin, her vocal cords retained—and for a brief time would continue to retain—the bivalent capacity to emit both sound and light. In fact, the phenomenon grew less frequent over time, as the newborn lived out its human fate and became an increasingly vile sinner.

Another decisive proof, according to Vredjuik, is the shot from a distant musket. If a musket is placed on top of a barrel or the roof of a house, and an observer several hundred paces away is positioned on top of another barrel or the roof of another house (in Holland necks are scarce), when the musket is fired—at night, for better results—the observer will see a small point of light. And then, after a not insignificant period of time, the noise of the shot will reach him. Obviously, the same phenomenon occurs in the two events, consistent with igniting a quantity of gunpowder. A portion of light, devoid of sin, instantly reaches the observer, whereas the contaminated portion—who knows how many hands touched that powder—arrives with difficulty, in the guise of a blast. By the same token, Vredjuik adds rather obscurely, the syphilitic walks with a cane.

Other examples of sinless light are: the stars, which pagans affirm are in the habit of making music, but which in Christian countries undoubtedly make none, no matter how intently the author listened to them in Udenhout on those endless nights when animals and rivers fell silent; the sun, from which one never hears a single peep, and the moon, notoriously mum; fog, which is always soundless; the lamps in Dutch Reformed churches (those in other churches emit a characteristic sputter); comets (Vredjuik admits that he never saw or heard a comet, but was told about them); the eyes of mute babies (the author's fourth son was mute); the renowned lighthouse of New Amsterdam, known today as New York, and generally the entire chain of lighthouses between Zeeland and Friesland; several benign varieties of ghosts and ignes fatui.

The book of the forgotten gravedigger from Brabant concludes with a "Warning to the Reader" concerning the essential immortality of noise, music, song, and conversation.

Charles Carroll

According to Charles Carroll of St. Louis, author of *The Negro a Beast* (1900) and *The Tempter of Eve* (1902), God created the African together with the animals for the sole reason that Adam and his descendants might not lack maids, dishwashers, bootblacks, bathroom attendants, and providers of similar services in the Garden of Eden. Like other mammals, the African manifests a species of intellect somewhere between dog and ape. But he is entirely devoid of soul.

The serpent who tempted Eve was in fact the first human couple's African maidservant. Cain, forced by his father and the circumstances to marry his sister, shunned incest and preferred to marry one of the dark-skinned apes or servants. From this hybrid marriage issued the various races of the earth. The white race, however, descends from another, more serious son of Adam.

Hence, all the descendants of Cain are, like their simian progenitor, without a soul. When the mother is African, the man cannot transmit even a trace of the divine spirit to his offspring. Therefore only whites get any at all. It occasionally happens that a mulatto learns to write, but, states Carroll, "the mere fact that Alexandre Dumas possessed a fine mind is no evidence that he possessed a soul."

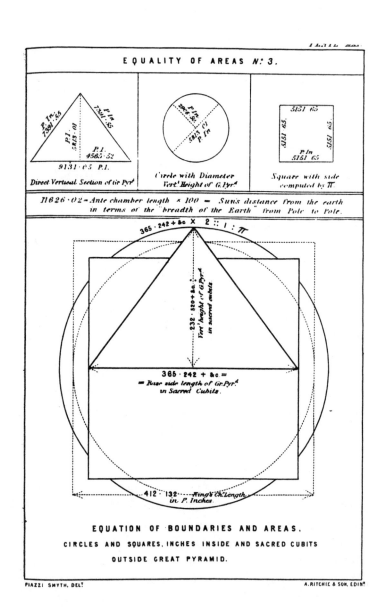

from *Our Inheritance in the Great Pyramid*, 1864

Charles Piazzi-Smyth

Near the end of the nineteenth century, the office of Astronomer Royal in Scotland was held by a professor at the University of Edinburgh called Charles Piazzi-Smyth. Piazzi-Smyth founded popular pyramidology with his 664-page tome, *Our Inheritance in the Great Pyramid,* published in 1864. Reprinted four times, this book was translated into nearly all the languages of Europe. In 1923, the Abbé Théophile Moreux, director of the observatory at Bourges and author of *Les Mystères de la Grande Pyramide,* was still speaking of it with enormous respect.

Immediately after the book's appearance, pleasurably impressed by its success, Piazzi-Smyth thought that the moment had arrived to travel to Egypt and take a glance at the object of his studies. No sooner had he descended from the camel, tape measure in hand, than he made a series of sensational discoveries. They were first presented to the public in 1867 in the three meticulous volumes of *Life and Work at the Great Pyramid* (his visit lasted only six months) and then a year later in the treatise *On the Antiquity of Intellectual Man.*

The three pyramids at Giza were originally encased in brilliant white limestone blocks, which were cut so finely as to be virtually seamless. The first thing Piazzi-Smyth discovered was that the base of the Great Pyramid, divided by the width of a casing stone, equaled exactly 365—the number of days in a year.

The discovery was actually a prophecy, since the first casing stones were unearthed in the course of excavations performed after Piazzi-Smyth's death. His admirers were also perplexed by the subsequent revelation that the stones varied in width.

Our Inheritance in the Great Pyramid enjoyed a readership in the millions and generated scores of other books, inevitably on the same topic. Its principal popularizer in France was the Abbé F. Moigno, Canon of St. Denis in Paris. In 1897 an International Institute for Preserving and Perfecting Weights and Measures was created in Boston. It aimed to modify the global system of weights and measures by establishing anew their conformity with the sacred parameters of the Great Pyramid. This revision entailed the abolition of the French metric system, which was charged with atheism. The supporters of the institute in question included James Garfield, president of the United States. During the 1880s a periodical called *The International Standard* was published, it too destined to advocate the return to Egyptian measurements. The most important measure—because from it derived almost all the others—was the pyramidal cubit.

The editor of *The International Standard* was an engineer who wrote: "We proclaim our eternal and incessant antagonism toward that immensely grievous disgrace, the French Metric System." The same issue printed the pæan to pyramidologists for the first time. It ended with the line: "Death to every metric scheme!"

In England, Joseph Seiss's *Miracle in Stone* (viz. the Great Pyramid) ran through fourteen consecutive editions. In 1905 Colonel J. Garnier published a book to announce that surveys which he himself had executed inside the Pyramid foretold Jesus Christ's return to earth in 1920. Walter Bynn made a similar prediction in 1926, but for 1932. When the sacred appointment was missed, Bynn published a new round of predictions in 1933, post-poning Christ's return for another few years.

The readers most deeply convinced by Piazzi-Smyth's book on the mysteries of the Great Pyramid included the preacher Charles Taze Russell of Allegheny, Pennsylvania, founder of the sect now known as Jehovah's Witnesses. Taze Russell published a multi-volume series of Biblical prophecies, partly based on Piazzi-Smyth's pyramidological discoveries. According to Reverend Russell, the Bible and the Pyramid of Cheops agreed in revealing that the Second Coming of Christ had already occurred, in se-cret, during 1874. This silent coming ushered in a forty-year pe-riod called the "Harvest," during which Jehovah's Witnesses were entrusted to the care and guidance of Reverend Russell. The cli-mactic episode in Russell's series predicted the Last Judgment for 1914. The dead will return to life and immediately be granted a second chance: whether or not to accept Jesus Christ. Those who refuse will be eliminated, and Evil will vanish from the world. Because the Witnesses accept, they will enjoy life eternal.

Two English brothers, John and Morton Edgar, were so struck by this prophecy that they rushed to Egypt to measure the Great Pyramid once again. Their measurements amply con-firmed Reverend Russell's prediction, as one can read in the two weighty volumes published by the Edgars in 1910 and 1913, *The Great Pyramid Passages and Chambers.* In 1914, however, the ma-jority of the dead abstained from coming back to life, and the sect lost thousands of adherents. The passage in the 1910 edition of Russell's book that read, "The deliverance of the saints must take place some time before 1914," was altered in the 1924 reprint to read, "The deliverance of the saints must take place very soon after 1914." In the meantime, Russell's successor was installed. The new leader of the Witnesses, seeking some way of solving the problem, decided that Jesus Christ did in fact return to earth in 1914, but chose not to speak to anybody. Beginning with that moment, called the Secret Coming, the Reign of Righteousness had resumed. For the time being, however, it was invisible.

Alfred Attendu

At Haut-les-Aigues, in a corner of Jura near the Swiss border, Dr. Alfred Attendu directed his panoramic Sanatorium for Reeducation, a hospice for cretins. The years between 1940 and 1944 were its Golden Age. In that period, he carried out undisturbed the studies, experiments, and observations that he subsequently gathered in his text, still a classic on the subject: *L'embêtement de l'intelligence* (Bésançon, 1945; The Insufferable Boredom of Intelligence).

Isolated, forgotten, self-sufficient, plentifully supplied with patients to reeducate, mysteriously spared any Teutonic invasiveness thanks to the disastrous condition of the only access road, which had been blown to smithereens by misguided shelling (the Germans believed it led to Switzerland because a sign read "Shelter for the Deficient")—in a word, king of his little kingdom of nitwits, Attendu could afford to ignore those years that the newspapers pompously called the collapse of a world. In reality, however, viewed from the height of History, or at least from the height of Jura, it was no more than a double change of police forces with a few settlement disputes.

The title of Attendu's book leaks his thesis: namely, that in every function and process which is unnecessary for vegetative life, the brain is a source of vexatious tedium. For centuries, current opinion held that idiocy in man is a symptom of degeneration. Attendu overturns this centuries-old prejudice and affirms that the idiot is nothing less than the primitive human prototype, of which we are simply the corrupt version and therefore subject to unnatural disturbances, passions, and manias which the true, unadulterated cretin is happily spared.

In his book, the French psychiatrist describes or posits an original Eden populated by imbeciles: dull, torpid, with porcine eyes, sallow cheeks, gaping lips, protruding tongue, drooling, deep, husky voice, hard of hearing, sex irrelevant. With classical eloquence, he calls them *les enfants du bon Dieu* (the Good Lord's children). Their descendants, improperly called men, increasingly deviate from the platonic model, or primigenial imbecile, because they are thrust toward the demented abysses of language and morality, work and art. From time to time, a fortunate mother is granted the privilege of bringing an idiot into the world, nostalgic image of the first creation, in whose face God is once again reflected. These transparent creatures are the mute testimony of our depravation; among us they wander like mirrors of the first divine stupidity. Man is ashamed of them, however, and shuts them away to forget them. Tranquil, the sinless angels enjoy brief lives of perpetual, uncontrolled joy, eating dirt, masturbating continuously, wallowing in mud, snuggling in the dog's amiable bed, unthinkingly sticking their fingers in the fire, defenseless, superior, invulnerable.

Any program to put the deficient back into civil society, whether their condition is congenital or accidental, is based on the assumption that we are the evolved and they the degenerates. This is patently false. Attendu reverses the assumption, decides that we are the degenerates and they the paragons, and thus sets going an opposite movement. Until now, and for very specific reasons, the only support enjoyed by this view was the ancient yet tacit collaboration of the greatest authorities, psychiatric and otherwise, who tend to exasperate in imbeciles precisely what renders them imbecilic.

Attendu did indeed have his reasons. From the height of Haut-les-Aigues he saw (metaphorically speaking, because he neither was an eagle nor possessed a telescope) the armies of both sides coming and going as in a comic film, pushing vast barriers of imperceptible air, shooting backward, fleeing toward victory, constructing to destroy, tearing down flags that cost very little at the cost of their lives. Their senseless bustling about exceeded human comprehension.

Yet turning his gaze in the opposite direction, within the confines of his sunny garden, Attendu saw his simpletons amidst the spruce trees. They too were twenty years old and full of life, playing games of ceaseless invention, like tearing a ball to pieces with their teeth, picking their noses with their mates' big toes, grabbing at the fish in the pond, turning on all the taps to see what would happen, digging a hole just to sit in it, ripping into strips the sheets hung out to dry and then running about and waving the strips in the air. Those who were more composed re-signedly filled their belly buttons with dung or, deep in reflection, tore out the hair from their heads one strand at a time. Even the smell of the original Garden must have been the same. The in-mates required protection, yes, but in their capacity as precious messengers, exemplary, fragile, touched—as was always said of them—by the Lord God, selected for companions by His Son.

The choice was fixed: anyone would choose the hospice nitwits. Nonetheless, Attendu's merit lay in drawing the proper conclusion from the choice: since the condition of cretinism is the ideal condition for the normal human being, he was deter-mined to study the diverse ways whereby imperfect cretins may achieve the desired perfection. In those years, the cognitively im-paired were classified according to their mental age, which can be inferred from the appropriate tests: a mental age of three years or less, idiots; from three to seven years, imbeciles; from eight to twelve years, morons. The scholar's goal was therefore to discover an effective means of reducing morons to the level of imbeciles and then imbeciles to complete idiocy. Attendu's various attempts in this direction, as well as the most pertinent methods, are described in detail in his interesting book, often cited in bibliographies. Curiously, few commentators have revealed that the etymological meaning of *embêtement* is brutishness.

The first treatment in the sanatorium consisted of abolishing the patient's contact with language. Since on admission internees might still possess some form of verbal communication, however rudimentary, the new arrivals were segregated in a cell or box until silence and darkness removed every remnant or suspicion of loquacity. In general, a few months sufficed. Dr. Attendu's expert nurses were capable of recognizing—from the nature of the pupil's grunts—when the moment arrived to drag him from the cubicle and lead him to the pigsty.

Pigsty therapy showed itself to be the most efficacious in reaching the next target, which was to remove from the boarder any trace of good manners, cleanliness, order, and similar subhuman characteristics previously and inevitably acquired. In this sense, the most difficult pupils proved to be the products of religious institutions, places that were in fact known for the scrupulous respect they paid to good manners and cleanliness. Those, however, who came directly from the bosom of their families—i.e., from a French bosom—spontaneously advanced to coarseness and filth.

Every boarder was supplied with a cudgel and periodically invited by the nurses to give his mates a good cudgeling. These therapies tended to eliminate every residue of social aggression from their mental void. Boys and girls also got used to wandering about naked, even in winter, and by means of illustrations they were induced to engage in bestial games of various sorts. This was particularly encouraged among the morons, who quite gladly participated in such games with the nurses. At the imbecilic stage, more so than at the idiotic, the instincts experience a refinement and regression to primitive purity: the most they could manage was eating one another's feces. But the morons, in their own way, tastefully abandoned themselves to a kind of giddy angelic sexual life.

At night, the sanatorium became the site of a great hubbub and was frequently transformed into a truly animated brothel. This proved to be a good sign because, according to the doctor, tranquil and prolonged sleep is a symptom of undue mental activity during the day. If at night, in fact, an internee was found in the anomalous state of deep sleep, the nurses pulled him from his bed and tossed him into a tank of cold water. Occasionally, some imbeciles intervened and tossed a nurse into the tank. The more evolved idiots, in contrast, stood at a distance, completely apathetic at this stage. Aristocrats, who were the doctor's favorites, referred to the idiots as the nurses. True and proper idiots took pleasure in movies more than anything else, especially color movies. But deafening noise also gladdened them, chiefly recordings of popular songs.

From 1946 onward, Dr. Attendu underwent various legal proceedings in the course of which another interesting scientific detail came to light. Nearly all the mental deficients found in the sanatorium at the age of one, two, or three years, the so-called *p'tits anges* (little angels), were his offspring, apparently produced *in loco* by artifical insemination. For the twenty-three young mothers, a maternity ward was constructed in the form of a cozy hen-house, paved in easily washable cement.

John O. Kinnaman

In 1938 John Kinnaman visited Sodom. On his return to England, he published *Diggers for Facts* (1940). In this book, he describes finding a site that contained numerous pillars and pyramids of salt. His discovery rendered rather difficult, not to say impossible, the task he initially set for himself: ascertaining which of these protrusions might be Lot's wife. He writes: "There are many actual pillars of salt in that region, but which may be the remains of that unfortunate woman, no one can tell."

The surrounding area yielded a compensation. Kinnaman unearthed the house where Abraham lived and, in the house, a stone whose surface was incised with the patriarch's signature: 𝔄braham.

Henrik Lorgion

Imagine a directory of ideal substances, long sought but never discovered. It would include H.G. Wells's cavorite, capable of abolishing the force of gravity; ground unicorn horn, which renders poisons innocuous; the liquid that effects invisibility, also from Wells; phlogiston, or the substance of fire, which instead of weight possesses lightness; Wilhelm Reich's bions, vesicles of sexual energy obtainable from sand; the philosopher's stone for the transmutation of base metals into gold or silver; dragon's teeth to ward off enemies; the ring of the Nibelungs, which endows its owner with power; the water from the fountain that drove Ponce de León to discover Florida by accident; Galen's four humours—hypochondriac, melancholic, choleric, phlegmatic—which turn the body into a battlefield and create hierarchies among themselves; the mind, which according to Durand Des Gros is a dense colony of tiny animals, whereas according to the latest theories it is a chemical substance that establishes contacts along synapses; the blood of Christ, collected in a cup by Joseph of Arimathea; and 114, an element that should be stable if current calculations are correct.

To this perhaps infinite list we must add another item from the research of Dr. Henrik Lorgion, an early nineteenth-century physician based in Emmen, Holland. For interminable years he sought—in both human and plant lymph, in flying fish import-ed from the colonies, in everything mutable—the substance of beauty.

Lorgion maintained that every perfect, harmonious, and symmetrical thing in nature derives its perfection, harmony, and symmetry from a volatile liquid he dubbed "eumorphine." It vanishes when life dies and forces the dead human, beast, or veg-etable to descend into disorder and disharmony. With every passing away, this substance seeps out of bodies into the sur-rounding elements, until the normal organic processes of living beings reabsorb it and beautify themselves anew. The idea ac-quires plausibility if one considers that every being is born clum-sy and gormless and only gradually draws form, color, and pro-portion from air, light, and food.

Far from the great research centers, Paris, Leyden, Vienna, Lorgion had access to no more than an antiquated microscope he bought in Amsterdam, a knowledge of chemistry that was no more than approximate—given the rudimentary state of this sci-ence in his epoch—and a stubborn conviction, utterly idealistic, that everything is or can be reduced to matter. Whatever he ex-amined in his apparatus, the Dutchman remained deeply im-pressed by the beauty of forms and the brilliance of colors. Infu-soria, hair, the eyes of insects, velvety mucous membrane, sta-mens and pistils and pollen, dewdrops, dewlaps, snowflakes, silicate crystals, the minute eggs of a spider, goose quills, newt skin—in his eyes they all bespoke a Maker, an Artist, an inex-haustible, infinitely inventive Aesthete, a composer of endless arrangements. And for Lorgion that Maker of substances could only be a substance as well.

Of course such ideas were not entirely original, since every-thing, or nearly everything, had already been stated by some

Greek. Reduced to its essence, however, Lorgion's theory challenged Ockham's razor, the principle of explanatory parsimony: "Entities are not to be multiplied without necessity." What another scientist took for a prism cut from Iceland spar, the doctor from Emmen called an alloy or combination of calcite and eumorphine. The mineral in itself was a shapeless mass; the eumorphine rendered it prismatic, transparent, colorless, glossy, birefractive—in a word, beautiful. Heated at a sufficiently high temperature, the two substances might separate, and in a crucible the crystal could always be reduced to an aneumorphous mound of powder. Yet to collect the eumorphine that evaporated in the process ... for that task Lorgion had not yet devised the proper instrument.

He tried with an alembic by calcining butterflies. But by the seventy-fifth *Papilium machaon* (swallowtail) he had distilled no more than a drop of liquid, dense and turbid, reminiscent of tar pits, visibly devoid of eumorphine. He tried by depositing a tulip in a hermetically sealed glass sphere, and strangely the tulip remained intact for a fairly long time. In the end, however, it collapsed into a heap of dust. Perhaps its beauty condensed on the inner surface of the sphere. Lorgion shattered the glass, but found nothing concrete.

These experiments, accompanied by a convincing explanation of their partial failure, are described in a long report printed at Utrecht in 1847, with the simple yet somewhat enigmatic title of *Eumorphion* ("enigmatic" in that the book must be read to understand the title). The volume is divided into 237 brief chapters, each of which is dedicated to a different experiment. Of the 237 tests, at least nine, in the author's assessment, yield a positive and tangible result: in total, seven drops of eumorphine, which were carefully preserved for nearly a century in a vial stored at the

Municipal Museum in Emmen. In 1940, eighty-two German bombs destroyed both vial and museum. The extract of beauty contained therein no doubt returned to nature, since beauty, according to Lorgion, is indestructible.

After the publication of the book (which wasn't very successful, perhaps because Emmen seemed so remote from the scientific world), Lorgion continued his research with tenacity. In 1851 he was sentenced, first to life imprisonment in an insane asylum, then to death by hanging, for calcining in a special copper boiler a fourteen-year-old boy whose trade was milking cows.

André Lebran

André Lebran is remembered, modestly remembered, actually not remembered at all, as the inventor of the pentacycle, or five-wheeled bicycle. Setting out from the universally familiar tricycle used in transport, one can easily imagine a similar mechanism with four instead of two wheels on the rear axle, making five altogether. A vehicle of this kind may in fact exist somewhere. Nothing, however, could be further from Lebran's intentions. A scholarly autodidact in mineralogy, he was possessed of a Pythagorical mind which took particular delight in polygons and perfect polyhedrals, sometimes called Aristotelian shapes, pure mental objects that have the property of having infinite properties. His pentacycle was, therefore, a pentagonal bicycle, and its seat was the center of the polygon with a wheel at every corner.

Obviously, if the wheels were arranged along a radial axis, or at tangents to one another, the vehicle would have been useless. In the second case, perhaps, it might have functioned like a mill wheel. Yet even overlooking the low efficiency of a pedal-driven mill, one certainly could not employ it as a vehicle. In Lebran's observation, the wheels in any means of transport that didn't revolve on itself tended to assume a parallel position. He also observed, vice versa, that as soon as one or more wheels were removed from this position, the vehicle revolved, or spun around a fixed point in the vicinity, or just fell motionless. Therefore, he sagely concluded, the five wheels of his pentacycle must all point in the same direction.

Having established this premise, he still had to face the fact that it was difficult to imagine a more pointless, cumbersome, and vain contraption. Or so at least Fate decreed in awarding him a second, definitive prize: oblivion. The first, a silver medal, was conferred on the occasion of the great Universal Exposition at Paris in 1889. In one of the pavilions, before the Palais des Machines, the pentacycle was first exhibited to the skeptical admiration of the French. And the inventor himself was perched on the seat, fitted with sturdy protective goggles.

Lebran was assigned to a small platform, a surface of sixteen square meters. When it was not raining, however, he was permitted to descend and ride a few times around the inner courtyard of the exposition. When it was raining, he was restricted to pedaling within the circumscribed ambit of his red-carpeted platform. There he could make trips that stretched for a meter, a meter and a half; when he reached the railing, he got off, pushed the mechanism another meter and a half, then got on again and recommenced. At certain moments, to alleviate the visitors' tedium, Lebran would appear in public dressed as a Seminole Indian.

From a leaflet that the inventor released on the occasion, we report the following explanatory notes. "Three supporting wheels, with front and back traction; the remaining two lateral wheels contribute to the overall balance. The axles are collapsible and adjustable, with sufficient flexibility to absorb the unevenness of the terrain. Minimal friction on ascent; speed on descent equal to that of an ordinary bicycle multiplied by factor K (K concerns the depth of mud and varies from 2 to 2½). Possesses remarkable military advantages as a replacement for the horse: no fodder needed, won't overturn on shell-riddled ground, little surface exposure to machine-gun fire, and the quincuncial design prevents a projectile from striking more than one wheel at a time. A solitary regiment on pentacycles could have serenely devastated the entire Marne valley in a single day. A logical development of the magical, exotic, and geometric properties of the pentagon, the pentacle, and the Pentateuch. Triple cork-lined brakes. The seat can be either widened or narrowed according to the size of driver. Hooks intended for the eventual addition of two (2) baskets to transport babies and wet nurses. The rolling can be regulated in the open country. Comes with parabolic mudguards. Equipped with as many as five (5) lamps for night journeys. A rear transversal litter can be attached beneath the seat to transport cadavers and the seriously ill. In the near future, the pentacycle will be utilized by the fire brigades in the city of Dijon (the fire-resistant aluminum model). Convertible into a pentaraft to negotiate ponds, floods, and tidal waves. Rapidly eliminates any form of obesity, whether mammary, abdominal, or gluteal. A sport vehicle that is especially decorous for young girls, married ladies, widows, and nurses. The Lebran pentacycle is fast but safe."

André Lebran's other inventions seem to have remained on paper. Three French patents from the early twentieth century bear his name. The most noteworthy is a fan consisting of a huge vertical triangle of light cardboard that is hung from the ceiling and activated from the bed with a cord.

Hans Hörbiger

Before the time of the moon we see in the sky today, the earth was orbited by six other moons, in succession, which directly caused the greatest cataclysms in its history. The vicissitudes of these seven moons are narrated in the 790-page volume entitled *Glazial-Kosmogonie*, written in 1913 by the Viennese engineer Hans Hörbiger with the help of an amateur astronomer. Abounding in photographs, diagrams, and demonstrations, the book subsequently gave rise to an astronomical cult whose loyal followers numbered in the millions. This particular German heresy was christened WEL, an acronym for *Welt-Eis-Lehre*, or Cosmic Ice Theory.

WEL quickly acquired the characteristics and proportions of a political party. It distributed fliers, posters, pamphlets; it issued numerous books and a monthly magazine, *The Key to World Events*. Disciples stormed into scientific conferences and interrupted speakers, shouting, "Out with astronomical orthodoxy! We want Hörbiger!" Hörbiger himself hurled his ideological challenge at the international community of astronomers. His corroboration consisted of a photograph in which he posed next to an eleven-inch Schmidt telescope, dressed enigmatically as a Knight of the Teutonic Order. The caption read: "Either with us or against us!"

According to WEL, since space is filled with rarefied hydrogen, satellites and planets tend to veer toward the center of rotation because hydrogen provides resistance that opposes their movement. Hence, the day will come when the entire solar system will wind up smack dab in the sun. In the course of this slow contraction, a heavenly body sometimes captures another, smaller body, turning it into a satellite. The history of the earth's satellites, especially the two most recent, can be inferred directly from the myths of ancient peoples. These myths constitute our fossil history.

The moon during the Tertiary geologic period, dating back 65 million years, was smaller than the one we presently possess. As this penultimate moon grew closer to the earth, the oceans heaved around the equator, and humankind took refuge wherever it could: Mexico, Tibet, Abyssinia, Bolivia. The worrisome object circled the earth in just four hours, six times a day; its unpleasantly pitted surface inspired the first legends about dragons and other flying monsters, including Milton's famous Satan.

Eventually, the force of earthly gravitation became so violent that the small moon started to crumble and the ice that covered it thawed, hurtling headlong onto the planet. Torrential rains fell, followed by ruinous hailstorms and finally annoying streams of stones and rocks, at which point the moon disintegrated completely. To these lunar aggressions the earth responded in its own way, preferring volcanic eruptions, until the oceans overwhelmed every continent—a documented event known as Noah's Flood.

From this disaster, as is written, a certain number of human beings were saved by clambering up mountains. There followed a happy era of true geologic peace, which the various myths of the Garden of Eden recall for us. But once again the earth was obliged to capture a moon, and once again it fell prey to paroxysms. This was today's moon, the worst of the lot.

Hans Hörbiger

The planet's axis shifted, the poles glaciated, Atlantis met the watery end that myths impart, and thus began the Quaternary period, 13,500 years ago. In *The Book of Revelation Is History*, Hans Schindler Bellamy, an English disciple of Hörbiger, demonstrates that the text attributed falsely to Saint John is nothing less than a detailed account of the catastrophe that closed the Tertiary period. And in his other book, *In the Beginning God*, he explains that Genesis does not describe the first creation of the world, but a more recent creation, if not the last, rendered necessary by the usual lunar drop. The author conjectures, moreover, that the legend of Adam's rib originated from a mere confusion of sexes, owing to the notorious imprecision of the first Hebrew copyists. It was actually a brief description of a cesarean section, performed under precarious sanitary conditions because of the chaos and disorganization that reigned at the time of Flood.

Hörbiger warned that the greatest imminent danger facing the earth is the moon, which one day or another will drop on our heads. This moon must be hard, furthermore, covered as it is with a layer of ice that is at least 200 kilometers thick. Mercury, Venus, and Mars are likewise covered with ice. The Milky Way, in fact, consists of gigantic ice blocks, certainly not stars, as the astronomers claim with their crudely doctored photographs.

WEL circulated widely and without refutation among the Nazis, who compared Hörbiger's intelligence to Hitler's, and Hitler's to Hörbiger's, both eminent sons of Austrian culture. Today, Cosmic Ice Theory commands only a few thousand adherents, like most of Austrian culture.

A. de Paniagua

A pupil of Elisée Reclus and friend of Onésime Reclus, A. de Paniagua wrote *La Civilisation Néolitique* to demonstrate that the French race was originally black and came from southern India—a view which does not deny that in an earlier epoch the French came from Australia, given the linguistic ties that Trombetti finds between Dravidic and primitive Australian. These blacks abandoned themselves to continuous migrations. Their first totem was the dog, as the root *kur* indicates, and therefore they called themselves Kurets. Since they traveled everywhere, one finds the root *kur* in many place names throughout the world: Kurlandia, Courmayeur, Kurdistan, Courbevoie, Corinth, Curinga in Calabria, and the Kurili Islands. Their second totem was the rooster, as the root *kor* indicates, and therefore they called themselves Corybantes. Place names that begin with "kor" or "cor"—Korea, Cordova, Kordofan, Cortina, Korca, Corato, Corfu, Corleone, Cork, Cornwall, Corno d'Oro, and Cornigliano Ligure—can also be found throughout the world, wherever the ancestors of the French may have traveled.

Such migratory enthusiasm is explained in part by what seems to be a verified fact: wherever Kureti and Corybantes arrived, whether in Scizia or in Scozia (evidently the same word), Japan or America, they turned white or yellow, as the need arose. Hence, the original French split into two large groups: the Kur, who were properly called dogs, and the Kor, who were roosters. Ethnologists have often confused the latter with dogs. Unfortunately, observes Paniagua, the reductive spirit tends to impoverish history.

Imagine, then, that dogs and roosters traverse the steppes of Central Asia, the Sahara, the Black Forest, Ireland. They are noisy, gay, intelligent—they are French. Two powerful cosmic forces move Kurets and Corybantes: the one to see where the sun rises, the other to see where the sun sets. Guided by these two impulses, opposed and unstoppable, they wind up circling the globe unwittingly.

Toward the east they withdraw, raving and frolicking, planting their menhirs along the road. They reach the Kurili Islands; another step, and they're in America. For confirmation one need only find the name of an important place that begins with Kur. The most obvious is Greenland, whose true name, Paniagua explains, must be Kureland. It would be mistaken to believe, however, that *Greenland* means "green earth," since Greenland is white, from whatever point of view one takes. Yet the ethnologist's winning card is a photograph of two Eskimos, evidently taken during the infinite polar sunset: they are in fact almost black.

Other Curets and Korybantes—likewise leaping and jostling, likewise dressed as dogs and roosters—set out toward the west. They venture up the Ister (today, the Danube), driven by a most sublime ideal. Deep in the dark blood of the race they already feel the joyous impulse to found France. As for their skin, upon passing through the Balkans, they turn white; some even become blond. At this point, they decide to assume the glorious name of Celts, so as to distinguish themselves from the blacks they left behind. The author explains that *Celt* means "celestial worshipper of fire," from *cel,* "celestial" (an immediate type of etymology) and *t* ("fire" in Dravidian, a mediated type of etymology).

While the new whites navigate up the Danube, Paniagua praises their patience and courage: so much travail, so many rivers and mountains to cross, all in order to lay the first stones in the edifice of light and splendor where the profound soul of France dwells immutable.

On the way, the Celts dispatch exploratory missions here and there, founding colonies that subsequently become illustrious— for example, Venice (the original French name is "Venise"), from the Dravidian *ven,* "white," and from the Celtic *is,* "down." It is difficult to find an etymology more exact, comments Paniagua. Yet another migratory break, and the Tyroleans fall away from the principal branch to establish themselves permanently on the coasts of the Tyrrhenian Sea, as the root *Tyr* indicates.

One more thick branch, losing patience with Switzerland for obstructing its path, sails down the Po and founds Italy (the original French name is "Italie"). The etymon is rather immediate in this case as well: *ita* comes from the Latin *ire,* "to journey," and *li* from the Sanskrit *lih,* "to lick." This means that the Kuret dogs do not only bark, but lick. Hence, *Italy* signifies "the country of migratory licking dogs." The point becomes even more evident if one thinks of the Ligurians, that mysterious people: "li-kuri," or licking dogs par excellence.

La Civilisation Néolitique (1923) was published by the firm of Paul Catin. Other volumes in the series include *Mon Artillerie* by Colonel Labrousse-Fonbelle and *Hellas, Hélas!* (memories of Salonika during the war) by Antoine Scheikevitch.

Benedict Lust

The inventor of zonal therapy was Dr. William H. Fitzgerald, for many years the senior nose and throat surgeon at St. Francis Hospital in Hartford, Connecticut. According to Fitzgerald, the human body is divided into ten zones, five on the right side and five on the left, each of which is directly linked to a digit of a hand and a corresponding digit of a foot. These linkages are too subtle to be detected with a microscope.

In 1917, Fitzgerald and a disciple by the name of Dr. Edwin F. Bowers published their fundamental treatise, entitled *Zone Therapy.* The authors affirmed that it is always possible to relieve the body of pain, and in many cases the illness itself, simply by pressing one digit of a hand or foot, or else some other peripheral area linked to the infected organ. This pressure can be applied in diverse ways. As a rule, one must bind the digit with a rubber band so tightly it turns blue; a clothespin can also be used. In certain special cases, it suffices to press the skin with the teeth of a metal comb.

Fitzgerald's theory was developed in the rather obstinately entitled manual *Zone Therapy,* the work of the esteemed naturopath, Dr. Benedict Lust. Lust's text, a useful supplement to Fitzgerald's homonymous treatise, offers detailed explanations of which digit must be pressed to overcome most of the illnesses that afflict humankind, not excluding cancer, polio, and appendicitis. Curing a goiter requires pressure on the index and middle fingers; but if "the goiter is very extensive, reaching to the fourth zone, it may be necessary to include the ring finger." With disorders of the sight, and of the eye in general, the index and middle fingers are likewise pressed. Deafness is cured, however, by pinching the ring finger or, better yet, the third digit of the foot. "One of the most effective means of treating partial deafness," Lust writes, "is to clamp a spring clothespin on the tip of the third finger, on the side involved in ear trouble."

Nausea is eliminated by exerting pressure on the back of the hand with a metal comb. Childbirth is rendered painless if the woman in labor firmly grasps two combs and squeezes them in such a way that the teeth press against the tips of all fingers simultaneously. The prospective mother will feel almost nothing at all if she takes the further precaution of tightly binding her big and second toes with a thin rubber band. With the same method, the dentist can forgo anesthesia: it is sufficient to apply a rubber band tightly around the digit of the patient's hand that is anatomically linked to the tooth to be extracted.

Hair loss can be combated with a method that Lust calls "simplicity itself." It involves "rubbing the fingernails of both hands briskly one against the other in a lateral motion for three or four minutes at a time." The operation is repeated several times a day to improve blood circulation and reinvigorate the scalp.

Henry Bucher

At the age of fifty-nine, the Belgian Henry Bucher was only forty-two. The reasons for this temporal contradiction can be read in the preface to his memoirs, *Souvenirs d'un chroniqueur de chroniques* (Liège, 1932; Memories of a Chronicler of Chronicles):

"Having obtained my degree and embarked with all the impetus of my green years on the delightful study of history, I soon realized that the task of locating, translating, and commenting on the entire corpus of medieval chroniclers—the obscure precursors of Froissart and Joinville, of the great Villehardouin and Commines—which I had set for myself as an absolute and preeminent pledge, exceeded the anticipated limits. Perhaps one life would be insufficient for me to bring it to a conclusion. Omitting the chore of searching for lost texts, in large part already completed—and admirably—by my revered teacher, Hébérard De la Boulerie, the mere process of translating from Latin to French (from an often bastard Latin to the elegant French of our time) would have required the entire arc of years that presumably the Fates were reserving for me. To this must be added the annotations, concordances (in this particular case, it would be much more just to call them discordances), the typing, as well as the various tasks relating to publication, proofreading, introductory essays, polemical exchanges, correspondence with various Academies, etc., not to mention the inevitable contingencies, and the reader will understand with what embarrassment and perplexity the young man I then was, on the threshold of twenty-five years, contemplated the enormous labor presenting itself to me, and the urgent need for a rational plan of work.

"The whole group of historical chronicles to be translated and annotated (excepting new discoveries, which were unlikely at this point but always possible) I already knew quite well and had acquired. Furthermore, I had imposed an additional limitation, that of concerning myself exclusively with works compiled between the ninth and eleventh centuries. The twelfth had already been mastered, perhaps a little too brilliantly, by my colleague Hennekin of Strasbourg; of the eighth, the Church was avariciously guarding the most promising pearls in its catacombs (*dans ses caves*). Even so, those lean three centuries would have cost me—according to calculations that were perhaps generous to a fault—at least thirty years of translation. If to this were added the remaining tasks, I would not crown the work before I reached eighty. To an ambitious and impatient young man, the static condition of an octogenarian can at times appear (without any rational basis, I daresay) scarcely attractive, and without lustre the laurels that unfailingly (although not always) adorn it. Thus things seemed to me then; I therefore contrived a means, if not of conquering time, then at least of restraining it.

"Already I had acutely observed that for a particularly active person, a week was insufficient to fulfill a week's obligations. The deferred tasks accumulate (replying to letters, filing papers and sorting socks, proofreading texts for the voracious press, without forgetting trips, weddings, deaths, revolutions, wars, and similar wastes of time). The cataract of days must be halted, at a certain point, to give one's complete attention to neglected duties. After which it would seem reasonable to set time in motion again, rid of arrears: free, revived, nimble, without aftereffects.

"And this I did, with the aid of my personal calendar. On a given day—let us say the 17th of July—I finished translating the Third Book of Ottone de Trier. I stopped the date; ipso facto I was free to type the manuscript, correct the proofs for the First Book, participate in person at the History Conference in Trieste, draft the Notes to the Second Book, hop over to the Sorbonne to foil some Apocrypha, bring my correspondence up to date, push on as far as Ostend by bicycle—and all this while holding firm the date of July 17th. At a certain point, no longer subject to obligations or constraints, I took up the Fifth Book and resumed my work. For other people, nearly two months had elapsed, and autumn was commencing; for me, in contrast, it was still July, precisely the 18th of July.

"Little by little I experienced the distinct sensation—corroborated by the facts—of lagging behind in time. When the Prussians invaded our beloved provinces, slitting the breasts of pregnant women and, what is worse, the electrical power lines, I was still fixed in 1905. For me, the war of 1914 ended in 1908. On the day that I finally reached 1914, my poor native land arrived at 1931 and passed through what they describe as an embarrassing economic crisis. I noticed, in fact, that every time I stopped the calendar the price of paper took a huge jump upward.

"Thanks to this process of taking my time, I manage to stave off weariness. I feel young; in truth, I am young. The historians who are my contemporaries are almost sixty, but I have only recently crossed the threshold of my forties. My simple expedient has proven itself to be doubly effective. Another ten, twelve years, and I shall have completed the work, the entire edition of

127 chronicles from three centuries in fluent modern French with an equally fluent commentary. At merely fifty years of age, I shall taste, if not glory, then the admired astonishment of my colleagues and—why not?—of ladies."

Luis Fuentecilla Herrera

In 1702, the microscopist Anton von Leeuwenhoek communicated a curious discovery to the Royal Society in London. In the stagnant rainwater that collects on roofs he found certain animalcules, which desiccated as the water evaporated but later, when reimmersed, returned to life.

> I found that once the liquid was consumed, the tiny animal contracted into the form of a miniscule egg and in this form remained immobile and lifeless until I covered it again with water as previously. After thirty minutes the creatures resumed their former appearance and could be seen swimming beneath the glass as if nothing had happened.

This phenomenon of latent life, obvious in seeds and spores, more spectacular in rotifers, nematodes, and bradypods, fascinated nineteenth-century speculators who viewed it as confirmation of the extreme vagueness—the extremely auspicious vagueness—of the boundary between life and death. Lenard H. Chisholm maintained, in *Are These Animals Alive?* (1853), that somehow we are all born from spores, and science is obliged to find a method of reducing us to our original state of sporedom, where we can be comfortably preserved for a millennium or two, finally returning to life inside a common bathtub.

In 1862, Edmond About brought out his novel *L'homme à l'oreille cassée* (The Man with the Broken Ear) in which the protagonist, a Napoleonic soldier, is dried out, packed away, then immersed in liquid fifty years later and revived exactly as he was at the moment of desiccation—except for an ear broken off during his lethargy. This pre-scientific novel enjoyed a huge success in Europe and was the cause, more than the effect, of interesting and durable reflections. Several years later, in 1871, the professor of natural sciences Abélard Cousin got hold of an Egyptian mummy recently disinterred at Memphis; and in the hope of catching a glimmer of residual life, he submerged it for approximately two months in the main cistern at the cloister of Saint Auban in Nantes. After two months of bathing the mummy was visibly full of worms, a species unknown till that day. At the very least, observed Cousin, this demonstrated that the Egyptians knew how to preserve their own worms.

The experiments proliferated. Between 1875 and 1885, no one could say how many cows, dogs, rabbits, rats, guinea pigs, hens, and horses were submitted to dehydration, still alive, over a slow flame in ovens of various kinds, in France, Belgium, Holland, Cuneo. The newspapers report the famous dried pig of Innsbruck, which made the rounds of the capitals in a traveling exhibition of monsters and various natural phenomena. The English, however, after the vigorous stand taken by the Society for the Protection of Animals, decided that this type of experiment was justified only with human subjects, "who possess the means to defend themselves," as the Society explained in notices that ran in the *Times* and other newspapers.

Even the French joined the English protest. Humans were too costly, except in the Balkans and Transylvania. And it seemed patently utopian to dry a corpse in the hope that after a few years it might come back to life. The subjects must be still living. The bey of Tunisia was known to offer death row prisoners at a reasonable price—but on the condition that once they were revived they would be immediately executed, voiding the research of any interest. In 1887, Louis Pasteur felt compelled to use the entire weight of his now unimpeachable authority to stop Dr. Sébrail from carrying out his plan: he had been permitted—and encouraged—by both the academic community and public health officials to collect the dying from Parisian hospitals solely for the purpose of desiccative experiments.

What Sébrail could not do in the tobacco drying rooms at Auteuil was done some years later by Dr. Fuentecilla Herrera at Cartagena in the Indies, notwithstanding the deliquescent heat, the pervasive humidity, the almost total lack of equipment, and the dearth of terminally ill subjects.

In fact, according to a turn-of-the century custom that was fairly widespread in Latin countries, especially those in America, the family of the sick refused to hand over their aspiring cadavers until they were seen exhaling their last breath. Of necessity, then, Luis Fuentecilla Herrera, director of the Hospital de la Caridad in Cartagena, was forced to experiment with sole-surviving septuagenarians admitted to the convent hospice, Asilo de Ancianos—raw material that was scarcely more promising than Cousin's mummies.

For dehyradation chambers Fuentecilla relied on the cabins used to dry leaf tobacco at the factory of La Universal Tabaquera, a business owned by one of his brothers. These facilities were, like the country itself, rather rudimentary. Because the product was destined exclusively for export, it was submitted to intense chemical treatment on its arrival in Europe, according to the most modern methods, but also because Colombian tobacco has always been stigmatized as mediocre.

It was calculated that between 1901 and 1905 Luis Fuentecilla

Herrera dehydrated fifty clinically alive geriatrics, male and female, in oblong cabins that were hermetically sealed and ventilated by a continuous air flow heated beforehand in special furnaces. Then came the arrest of his brother, who was denounced by his employees, and the scientist was forced to flee to New Orleans, which in those years was a notorious den of criminals and where he too probably turned to a life of crime. In the interval, he apparently married a black woman who spoke only a local dialect of French.

His candidates for experimental longevity were of two types, and the type dictated their behavior during the drying process. In the dry heated air, those who were more robust and vital putrefied rapidly and burst almost immediately, causing great inconvenience to the employees who tended to the leaves and cleaned the rooms. The other type, thin at the start, already shrunk by a life of hardship, grew increasingly slender and light, so that after two weeks they were easily lifted with the shovel used to handle the tobacco, wrapped up tightly in oiled paper, and stacked in a storeroom at the shipping warehouse, kept pleasantly dry, close to the harbor.

These bundles returned to the tobacco factory every three months for a second or third dehydration, just to be safe, a precaution rendered necessary by the climate, the rats, the insects, and the importance of the experiment. Specimens and subjects that spoiled were reconsigned to the nuns of the Asilo, whose confessor, luckily, served as the chaplain of the hospital under Fuentecilla's direction. And there, in the little cemetery next to the convent, the deceased can be found in loving sacks and worthy burial. Nevertheless, the nuns disposed of many elderly who were true and proper Indians, when they weren't simply Venezuelans.

Luis Fuentecilla Herrera

To the news of his brother's arrest Fuentecilla responded with a desperate attempt to demonstrate the soundness of his theories. He had twelve of the better preserved specimens carried to the wharf and ordered them to be dunked in water, all twelve, each suspended from a rope. He hoped that at least one or two would come back to life, justifying his work, if not in his own country, then abroad. Yet the only thing he saw was the fish, all the fish in the harbor of Cartagena, who left nothing but the dangling ropes.

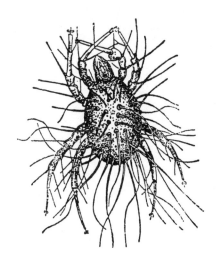

from *Oddities: A Book of Unexplained Facts,* 1928

Morley Martin

In 1836, while the Englishman Andrew Crosse was executing electrical experiments on a mixture of ground minerals, he was agreeably surprised to witness the birth of minute insects. This is what Crosse saw through the microscope:

> On the fourteenth day from the commencement of this experiment I observed through a lens a few small whitish excrescences or nipples projecting from about the middle of the electrified stone. On the eighteenth day these projections enlarged, and struck out seven or eight filaments.... On the twenty-sixth day these appearances assumed the form of a *perfect insect,* standing erect on a few bristles which formed its tail. Till this period I had no notion that these appearances were other than an incipient mineral formation. On the twenty-eighth day these little creatures moved their legs. I must now say that I was not a little astonished.

Thus he observed the birth of myriad mites. No sooner had the mites been born than they abandoned the microscope and flew about the room, concealing themselves in the dark nooks. Once the event was reported, another microscopic researcher (a man called Weeks who lived in Sandwich) wished to replicate the result, and he too obtained hundreds of mites. The details of the stupefying experiment can be read in three works: *Memorials, Scientific and Literary, of Andrew Crosse, The Electrician* gathered by a relative in 1857; *The History of England during the Thirty Years' Peace: 1816–1846* by Harriet Martineau (1849); and *Oddities: A Book of Unexplained Facts* (1928) by Lieutenant Commander Rupert T. Gould.

In 1927, in his private laboratory at Andover, the Englishman Morley Martin calcined a piece of Archaeozoic rock until it was reduced to ash. From this ash, by means of a complicated and secret chemical process, he subsequently derived a certain portion of primordial protoplasm. Carefully shielding it from air contamination, Martin submitted the substance to the action of X-rays. In the optical field he saw gradually emerge a fabulous quantity of living, microscopic plants and animals. Especially tiny fish. In a few square centimeters, the scientist succeeded in counting fifteen thousand fish.

This obviously meant that the organisms remained in a state of suspended animation for at least a billion years—which is to say from the Archaeozoic era to 1927. The disturbing discovery was made public in a short study entitled *The Reincarnation of Animal and Plant Life from Protoplasm Isolated from the Mineral Kingdom* (1934). To this discovery the writer Maurice Maeterlinck devotes a chapter of his book, *La Grande Porte* (1939). Today Martin's pamphlet is well-nigh unobtainable, but a description of the noteworthy experiment can be read in Maeterlinck's volume. We quote here from the English version that appeared in a 1948 mimeograph published by the Borderland Science Research Associates of San Diego:

> Under the enlargement of the microscope globules were seen taking shape within the protoplasm and forming vertebrae which elongated into a spinal column in which the ribs

were inserted; then came the outlines of the limbs or claws, the head, and the eyes. These transformations are normally slow and require several days, but at times they took place under the eyes of the observer. One crustacean, for example, having developed its legs, walked off the field of the microscope.

These emergents therefore live, sometimes move, and develop as long as they find sufficient nourishment in the protoplasm in which they were born: after that, their growth is checked or else they devour one another. Morley Martin has, however, succeeded in feeding them by the help of a serum whose secret he kept ...

Unfortunately, Morley Martin's discovery could not be replicated. It was well received by theosophists, particularly because it confirmed Madam Blavatsky's theory about the archetypes of primordial life, which originated on the earth during the period of fire and vapors but later, through the evolutionary process, developed into the forms we know today. Some years ago, following in Martin's footprints, Wilhelm Reich discovered in warm Norwegian sand a vast number of blue vesicles, which were not simply alive, but swollen with sexual energy. He called them "bions." These bions create clusters and finally evolve into protozoa, amoebas, and paramecia, consisting solely of desire, pulsating with libido. See Wilhelm Reich, *The Cancer Biopathy* (1948).

Yves de Lalande

Nobody today reads the novels of Yves de Lalande. And this peculiar fact breeds the suspicion that in the not too distant future nobody will read any novels at all. Yves de Lalande was a pseudonym: his real name was Hubert Puits. He was the first producer of novels on a truly industrial scale. Like everyone else, he started his activity on an artisanal level, turning out novels on a typewriter. With this method, however illustrious or primitive it might be, he required at least six months to conclude a work, and this work could scarcely be described as a finished product. In time, Puits became aware that the idea of writing on his own something as complex and varied as a novel, so rich with diverse moods and situations and viewpoints, seemed a task better suited to a Robinson Crusoe than a citizen of the greatest and most advanced industrial nation of the twentieth century: France.

To begin with, the editor of the Bibliothèque de Goût, for whom Puits was working at the time, demanded that his novels abound not only with adventures, but with scenes of romantic love. For six years, however, Puits had entertained an utterly normal relationship with his maid or housekeeper, a gray, miserly ex-nun who failed to inspire in him the slightest hint of romance. Hence, he was forced to extract it from books, and there was always something that didn't work. For example, when one of his heroines learned that she was the illegitimate daughter of the

French king's brother, she drew her fiancé's sword and pierced her breast. Yet the scene unfolded in the métro between Bac and Solferino, beneath the Ministry of Public Works—which might have seemed strange.

As for the adventures, once he happened to get stuck in an elevator for two and a half hours, and this episode frequently reappeared in his novels, even in one with a Chinese setting, *The Wild Beast of Cochin-China.* But he knew he couldn't exploit it ad infinitum. Puits was convinced that one man would not suffice to produce a good novel, that it would take ten, perhaps twenty. He thought of Balzac, Alexandre Dumas, Malraux. Who knows how many employees they had?

Yet men are given to quarreling among themselves: better to employ five men of good character than ten incompatible geniuses. Thus it was that Lalande's novel factory got off the ground. Here we shall describe not the successive phases of its development, but rather its peak operation, which, between 1927 and 1942, permitted the still youthful Marquis de Lalande (the title was also invented) to publish 672 novels, eighty-four of which were transposed to the screen with varying success.

The manufacturing process was rigorous, immutable. The workers were all healthy, mentally nimble girls, little inclined to self-assertion. When one of them showed signs of wishing to insert her own literary or otherwise individualistic aspirations into the mechanism of production, she was inexorably replaced. Together they took pride in the finished product. Nevertheless, the product was rarely one that could inspire the slightest pride, and in reality each of them worked, as was appropriate, for the salary, which was also appropriate.

Neither the praise nor censure nor silence of the critics touched the isolated walls of the petit-hôtel in Meudon, where

the novel factory was located. Contracts for publication, print-
ings, rights, translations were all handled by the office designed
for this purpose in rue Vaugirard. The villa in Meudon was entirely dedicated to creation; inside it whirred a single mind. That
house was a Balzac, an Alexandre Dumas, a symbiotic Malraux,
a literary colony, a Medusa. All the employees harmoniously
formed the body of Yves de Lalande.

In his capacity as owner-director of the firm, Hubert Puits
proposed every theme. The head of the Office of Basic Plots selected a plot suitable to the theme, updating it according to the
reigning style; this choice ranked among the most compelling
because it functioned more as an anticipation than a duplication
of the style. The head of Characterization received the plot and
accurately inferred the characters according to the proven for-
mulas; then she conveyed them to the Office of Individual Stories and Destinies.

Destinies performed a combinatory role: the head made use
of a roulette wheel, and for each character she drew three numbers corresponding to three index cards in the file of Basic Incidents, with which their destinies were rapidly composed. In the
Office of Reconciliations, the individual destinies were reconciled, so as to prevent a character from marrying his son, or from
being born before his father, or other, similar anomalies. The
Circumstances, now composed and reconciled, proceeded to the
expert in Basic Styles who assigned the most suitable style to the
novel, making her choice from among those in vogue at the moment. Finally, the girl assigned to Titles suggested from six to
eight titles, one of which would be selected when the work was
completed. This initial, preparatory phase required at most a
morning's work; immediately afterward the novel entered the
phase of true and proper Manufacture.

This phase was the most serious, but at the same time the most inflexibly automated and least contingent of the entire manufacturing process. The so-called Scenario was conveyed to the expert in Graphs, a recent graduate in Projection and Programming, who through a shrewd use of various graphs—temporal, spatial, motivational, and so forth—coordinated the entire event into systems of numbered Scenes, both sequential and parallel. From here the work, thus schematized, proceeded to the department of Scenes and Situations.

Scenes and Situations occupied the entire first floor and part of the attic of the villa in Meudon. It constituted an enormous, constantly growing Archive of scenes and situations for any number of characters, narrated in the first or third persons, with dialogue, action, description, introspective passages, and similar narrative elements. These scenes, each four to eight pages in length, were catalogued and arranged according to the most modern methods of classification, which allowed for their almost immediate retrieval. A gang of young bungling arts graduates constantly replenished the firm's already considerable archive with new scenes and situations, in compliance with the laws of the market. And four especially quick-witted girls were assigned to various jobs of research and classification.

As soon as the archivists received the scheme of numbered Scenes and Situations—let's say eighty, which made a novel of 450 to 500 typewritten pages—they proceeded to research pertinent treatments. They printed a copy of every scene, with the copying apparatus then in use, as cumbersome as it was efficacious. Then they arranged these copies in sequence, at which point the novel could indeed be called mounted.

Naturally, the product was still unrefined. For example, in every scene and situation the same character might appear with a different name, the provisional name originally assigned to him by the anonymous narrator. Two other girls were installed permanently in the attic from where, moreover, a splendid vista of the railroad and environs could be enjoyed. It was they who proceeded to apply the finishing touches.

The first of this duo, humorously dubbed the Iron by her colleagues, adjusted the names of people and places, smoothed out the inconsistencies, and linked the scenes together (subsequently, as tastes changed, this labor of linkage became unnecessary). At the same time, a young typist prepared a fresh typescript of the so-to-speak ironed text. The second girl, named Mimetica for her skill in imitating the style of any living writer with good sales figures, corrected the whole according to directions already established by the ground-floor Style Office. In reality, her task was much less arduous than it might have seemed; at most it required a quantity of detachment and artfulness sufficient to recognize that each writer's style is distinguished by a small number of simple obstinacies, foibles, affectations contracted in childhood, if not in old age, but nonetheless susceptible to imitation, whereas a plain, impersonal style is granted to few, and not of course to a best-selling writer.

As far as the dialogue was concerned, Mimetica completed Iron's work, properly bringing the protagonists' speech into line, independent of their social status, nationality, dialect, age, sex, occupation, and so forth. Yves de Lalande disapproved of local color, and rightly so.

At this point, the novel was virtually finished, so it was now consigned to the Grand Consultant, a mature woman with vast experience and a singular memory. She constituted a sort of living library in the sense that not only had she read every novel produced by the Lalande firm, but what is even more incredible, she remembered them. The Grand Consultant removed possible coincidences in the characters' names which might induce the reader to think that the character had already appeared in another novel by the same author. She was careful that situations were not used too often, or at any rate that they hadn't been employed in the firm's novels in the last three years, the maximum period attributed to the reader's memory by the experts. In a word, she gave a final buff to the product before stamping it approved and putting it into circulation. The entire assembly process, from the choice of the theme to the delivery of the typescript to the interested publisher, required no more than twenty days' work. If necessary, a mere two weeks at a steady pace could do the trick.

Yves de Lalande didn't read his own novels. As everyone knows, he was crushed to death against a plane tree in April of 1942, thrown from an automobile on his return from a light supper at Versailles with a group of jolly Wehrmacht officials. When the army of Liberation arrived, led by Jean-Paul Sartre, the literary journals in power decreed a ban on all the works of the petit-hôtel in Meudon—for collaborationism. Today the building is leased by the Society for the Protection of Animals, and they report that it is filled to the rafters with cats. Thus, in the native land of Balzac, Alexandre Dumas, and Malraux, a powerful intellect falls into decay.

Socrates Scholfield

God's existence has always raised doubts. The problem has occupied St. Thomas, St. Anselm, Descartes, Kant, Hume, Alvin Plantinga. Not the least of this group was Socrates Scholfield, holder of the patent registered with the U.S. Patent Office in 1914 under the number 1.087.186. The apparatus of his invention consists of two brass helices set in such a way that, by slowly winding around and within one another, they demonstrate the existence of God. Of the five classic proofs, this is called the mechanical proof.

Philip Baumberg

In 1874, near Wanganui in northern New Zealand, Philip Baumberg, an Irish native from Cork, first operated his canine-powered pump, or dog pump. The device, if such it can be called, exploited the scientifically demonstrated fact that a well-trained dog will come when it is summoned. Baumberg availed himself of some thirty work dogs, shepherds and similar breeds, and hired two indigenous laborers, whose number thereafter increased progressively.

The first laborer was positioned at the foot of a hill, with a bucket, near a stream of drinkable water; the second stood at the top, next to a wide metal pipe that was slightly inclined so as to conduct the water to a cistern adjacent to Baumberg's dwelling. Around each dog's neck hung a bucket that was filled by the aboriginal below. Then the one above called the dog, whose bucket of water was poured into the cistern pipe upon arrival. Immediately afterward, the aboriginal below called back the dog and repeated the operation.

With thirty dogs in action, the effect was especially animated. To avoid frequent errors caused by the impossibility of remembering the names of all thirty animals—errors that negatively affected the progress of the work (sometimes a dog summoned back too quickly returned with a full bucket)—Baumberg decided to separate the tasks. So the Maori now increased to four: two assigned to the pouring and two to the summoning. Later, to prevent the dogs from stopping on the hillside or leaving to go about their own business, he was required to add two more workers as guards along the slope.

Yet another two aboriginals were engaged to change the dogs, since normally the animals' particular nature and constitution did not permit them to work more than an hour at a stretch. Consequently, the actual number of dogs employed on the pump reached almost ninety, a development that so complicated the memorization of their names that two more Maori were recruited as auxiliaries to assist in the summoning. Four more aboriginals sought to prevent the dogs from biting each other, from abandoning themselves to indecencies, and above all from running away with the buckets, which were highly valued among the population of the interior, then as today.

Baumberg didn't overlook the obvious fact that if fourteen people were directly responsible for transporting the buckets, instead of performing animal surveillance and governance, they'd have carried a hundred times more water than thirty tail-wagging, capricious dogs. (Often the dogs just sat around scratching themselves, or played dead, while the most cunning and ancient among them ably simulated aches with their paws, fainting fits, and dizziness, especially the females.) Yet humanitarian considerations of an evangelical character—perfectly understandable in an Irish Jew in close contact with the gaunt but overbearing Catholic missionaries on the island—induced him not only to prefer animal labor, but to describe its advantages minutely. These can be read in his lone, rambling dissertation, *Dog as Worker: His Preeminence over Ass, Ox, and Man,* printed at Sydney in 1876.

Since a standard Patents Office didn't then exist in Auckland or any of the nearby settlements, and since not even Australia—

in good part still populated by the children and grandchildren of convicts—offered any special guarantees in this respect, Baumberg was forced to wait until his 1884 journey to London to patent his dog pump. Nonetheless, the invention and its specifications yielded him nothing but scorn and oblivion. Only Brewater speaks of it, in his exhaustive history of the forms of labor: *From the Pyramids to On-Line Surveillance,* the first volume of the *Enciclopedia del sindacalista* (Bari, 1969; The Trade Unionist's Encyclopedia).

SECTIONAL VIEW OF THE EARTH.

SHOWING THE
OPENINGS AT THE POLES.

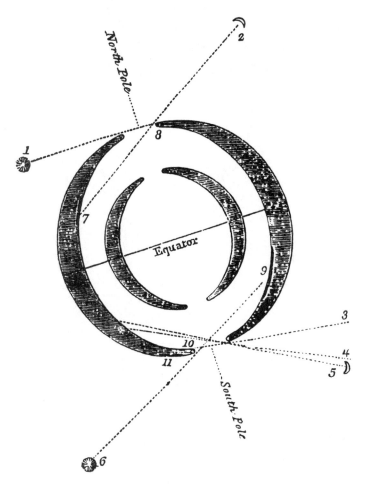

from *Symzonia*, 1820

Symmes, Teed, Gardner

Captain John Cleves Symmes maintained that the earth was made of five concentric spheres, all of which were perforated at the poles. For many years, the United States simply buzzed about this polar opening, commonly called "Symmes's Hole." In 1818 the captain widely distributed a leaflet wherein he explained how things stood and solicited the help of a hundred "brave companions" willing to explore with him the north hole, several thousand miles in diameter. Through the polar openings the sea flowed continuously onto the internal spheres, which abounded in plant and animal life.

Symmes's theories are expounded in two books, very different from each other, although both entitled *Symmes' Theory of Concentric Spheres*. The first was published in 1826 by a disciple, the second in 1878 by his son, Americus Symmes. Among the reasons Symmes adduced in support of his hypothesis is the point—obvious in his eyes—that the system of concentric spheres saved the Creator a considerable quantity of matter without greatly damaging the solidity of the whole. Moreover, the fact that the earth is inhabitable both inside and out must carry advantages for God, supreme landlord of the planets, that are economical as well as ecumenical.

Edgar Allan Poe's unfinished *Narrative of Arthur Gordon Pym* was apparently intended to describe a voyage to the center of the earth through Symmes's hole.

ONE NIGHT in 1869, sitting in his alchemical laboratory in Utica, Cyrus Reed Teed had a vision which he subsequently described in his pamphlet *The Illumination of Koresh: Marvelous Experience of the Great Alchemist at Utica, New York*. In the vision, a beautiful woman appeared to him and announced that he, Cyrus Teed, was destined to be the new Messiah. Before disappearing, she also explained to him the real structure of the universe, the key of the true cosmogony.

The key lies in the fact that the earth is a hollow sphere which contains the universe. Enclosed within this space, the increasingly smaller orbits of the heavenly bodies deceive astronomers by creating the illusion of infinity. Infinity is nothing more than the invisible center of the sphere.

Teed developed this revelation and in 1870, under the pseudonym of Koresh (the Hebrew equivalent of Cyrus), he published *The Cellular Cosmogony*. The entire universe is comparable to an egg. We live stuck to the inner surface of the shell. Suspended inside the hollow of this egg are the sun, moon, stars, planets, and comets; around these bodies circulate the sky and clouds. Outside is nothing, absolutely nothing. Near the center of the egg, however, the atmosphere is so dense that not even the most powerful telescopes enable us to see the antipodeans, who throng unaware on the opposite surface of the shell. The shell is one hundred miles thick and consists of seventeen strata. The first five, counting from the surface of the earth to the exterior nothingness, are geologic; then come five mineral strata and finally another seven of pure metal.

The sun, fixed in the center of the sphere, is in reality invisible: we perceive only a reflection of it. This invisible sun is half light and half dark. It spins on its axis, and from this rotation spring day and night, always by reflection. The moon too is a reflection, but of the earth itself. The planets, however, are reflections of "mercurial discs floating between the laminae of the metallic planes." Consequently, the heavenly bodies we see are not material, but rather focal points of light or, more precisely, virtual images.

Cyrus Teed was willing to admit that at first sight the earth seems to be convex. But this is obviously an optical illusion. One need only trace a horizontal line long enough to realize that sooner or later the line will run up against the upward curvature of land or sea. The experimental demonstration for this new law of optics was performed in 1897 by the Koreshan Geodetic Staff, who carried out the necessary survey on the gulf coast of Florida. They employed a set of three double T squares, an instrument that Teed called a "rectilineator." Subsequent editions of *The Cellular Cosmogony* contain a photograph showing the staff scientists at work, bearded, distinguished, ready to plunge their squares—at just the right moment—into the clear blue waters of the Gulf of Mexico. In point of fact, Teed explains, every time they tried to trace a line parallel to the horizon, after a brief journey of three or four miles, the line wound up in the water.

Cyrus Teed's style is nearly as extraordinary as an art critic's. The planets, he writes, are "spheres of substance aggregated through the impact of afferent and efferent fluxions of essence." The comets are "composed of cruosic force, caused by condensation of substance through the dissipation of caloric units at the opening of the electromagnetic circuits, which closes the conduits of solar and lunar energy." The author does not forget to compare himself to Harvey and Galileo.

Backed by four thousand followers who were equally convinced that the earth is a hollow sphere of which we know only the interior, the alchemist from Utica was consistently successful in arranging paid speaking engagements along the California coast. At the height of his zeal, he proclaimed that

> to know of the earth's concavity ... is to know God, while to believe in the earth's convexity is to deny Him and all his works. All that is opposed to Koreshanity is Antichrist.

Having accumulated great wealth, Teed acquired a tract of land in Florida and founded the city of Estero, otherwise called the New Jerusalem, the capital of the world. Estero was planned to accommodate a population of eight million, but when it was ready to welcome them, only two hundred arrived, making the New Jerusalem the least densely populated capital in the world. Teed died several years later. In another of his books, *The Immortal Manhood,* he predicted that he would rise again after his physical death, and the angels would transport him to heaven with all his disciples.

When his hour arrived, on the 22nd of December 1908, following a personal assault by the marshal of Fort Meyers, the members of the colony stopped working and kept vigil, praying and singing over the corpse. By Christmas Eve, Koresh stank; by the next day, the stench grew intolerable, but the faithful continued to wait for his resurrection. On the 26th, Koresh burst, and the authorities were forced to seize the remains and have them buried somewhere.

Teed's theories enjoyed a wide circulation throughout the civilized world. In Germany they gave rise to a cult called *Hohlweltlehre,* or Hollow Earth Doctrine, which achieved great popularity under Hitler's regime. Karl E. Neupert, its principal advocate, was imprisoned in a Nazi concentration camp for scientists and duly incinerated. The *Hohlweltlehre* moved to Argentina, where in 1947 the lawyer Duran Navarro succeeded in demonstrating that the force of gravity is actually centrifugal force generated by the rotation of this empty shell, on whose rough surface we live and die.

In 1913, the mechanic Marshall B. Gardner of Aurora, Illinois, published his sixty-nine-page work *Journey to the Earth's Interior; or, Have the Poles Really Been Discovered?* The author worked in a corset factory. Even though he maintained, like Symmes, that the earth was a hollow sphere, he spent his entire life denying that he was inspired by his predecessor's ideas, which he professed not to know. In 1920, Gardner enlarged his book to 456 pages and added photographs. Here the mechanic from Aurora explicitly rejected Symmes's theory of the five concentric spheres, declaring it a "fantastic notion." The earth was hollow, yes, but it consisted only of a heavy shell, 800 miles thick. The rest was sky.

In the center of this enclosed sky, a sun 600 miles in diameter eternally illuminates the interior surface. Both poles feature huge openings, each 1,400 miles wide. The other planets are constructed in the same fashion. Close observation of Mars is sufficient to perceive the two large openings, which are lit by the interior Martian sun. On the earth, the light streaming from the opening at the North Pole causes the aurora borealis in the arctic region.

The mammoths discovered in Siberia came from the interior of the earth, where they continue to thrive, placid as well as fertile. The Eskimos also came from the interior. "Truly it is most strange," observes Gardner, "that no expedition to the North Pole has yet managed to find the opening, an orifice of such vast dimensions." Right up to his death he questioned the integrity (or at least the eyesight) of Admiral Richard Byrd, the first to fly over the North Pole.

Gardner's disciples are still active, working busily to disseminate and perfect his teachings. They publish illustrated books like Raymond Bernard's *The Hollow Earth* (1969), which depicts the interior as a place where the temperature remains a pleasant 29 degrees centigrade, and a highly evolved race constructs the flying saucers that we periodically see issue from the north hole. The theory concerning the subterranean origin of flying saucers was propounded in the 1950s by O.C. Huguenin (see his book *From the Subterranean World to the Sky*). The credit for this conjecture, however, belongs to Henrique José de Souza, president of the Theosophical Society of Minas Gerais in Brazil and counsel for the grandiose Greek temple in São Lourenço which is dedicated to the mysteries of the lower world.

Niklaus Odelius

For a moment, around 1890, the enemies of Darwinism were threatening to drag Europe toward a new heresy, so attractive as to seduce even the Church Militant. They were tempted to adhere to the theories of Niklaus Odelius, professor of zoology at Bergen and correspondent with the Royal Institute for the Sciences at Königsberg. The temptation, however, proved as ephemeral as the theory.

Like many other scholars in his century, Odelius arrived at the conclusion that the creation story left to us by Moses required a thorough revision. Not in fact because the account in Genesis was not inspired by God Himself, but because the written expression of that inspiration had been entrusted to the Hebrew language. Now, a characteristic of Hebrew writing is that it appears to be reversed—or at least it reads in the direction that the world unanimously considers reversed, i.e., from right to left. This served as a means (one among the many excogitated by God, that Eternal Wit) of signaling to readers that the events described therein were also reversed. Generations have asked themselves how on earth did God separate light from darkness one day and then, several days later, create the sun and stars that constitute the only known sources of light. Odelius responded simply that the sun was created before light, and man before the beasts. This involved curious consequences.

Like all naturalists of his period, Odelius was an evolutionist. Yet among his contemporaries he was unique in continuing to maintain, as many in the sixteenth and seventeenth centuries had maintained, that evolution implied a decline, not only from a state of original perfection, verifiable to a greater or lesser extent in various species both extinct and extant, but also a decline along the biological scale, from species to species, from God's most ancient and supreme invention, which is man, all the way down to the most modern protozoa. Man afflicted with the primigenial sin became ape (not all men, however, since some still retain their original state, testifying to the glory of the Creator), ape became polecat, polecat became sperm whale, and so on from geckos to fish, fish to calamari, calamari to hydras, hydras to amoebas. From the very beginning, the world took a bad turn.

Niklaus Odelius, zoologist, conjectured that something similar must have happened with plants. But he left that aspect of the problem to the botanists. He recognized that the text of the creation was at times decidedly boustrophedonic, or rather that some things happened later and some before, with respect to the way they were narrated or treated as evidence in the fossil record. The particulars, however, didn't concern him. What he found most intriguing was the grand synthesis, the organizing principle, the clever intuition that not only made the arrogant gang of Darwinists bite the dust, but cast an unwonted light on the twisted millennia of the creation, the descent from Adam to baboon, dog, elephant, pterodactyl, serpent. In contrast, Eve descended into gentle, feminine creatures, suggested Odelius, plush beavers, gorgeous birds, precious tortoises. The idea that the tortoise was a precious animal, and hence comparable to a woman, may seem arbitrary today. But it was widely held at the close of the last century, when she (the tortoise) was used in the manufacture of combs, eyeglasses, and snuff boxes.

Niklaus Odelius

A scholar capable of affirming that camels descended from the Arabs could perhaps keep himself afloat in the Middle Ages. Yet if he were a scientist eighty years ago, his reputation would be doomed to rapid extinction. Official science is a citadel in whose corridors battles sometimes, perhaps always, rage. But its gates don't open at the first knock. *From Genesis to the Microbe* (1887), the work in which Odelius presented the most articulate formulation of his theory concerning the progressive stultification of the species, could have been greeted with curiosity, skepticism, repugnance, hilarity. It was not, however, greeted at all. It sank like a stone into the cesspool of scientific sewage. No one took the trouble to refute it, the clearest sign of scorn among scientists. This reception did not drive Odelius to suicide. In the solitude of obstinacy, he lived long enough to be granted the sight of the Nazis' arrival at Bergen, as if to confirm his perpetually repudiated theory.

Llorenz Riber

Llorenz Riber enjoyed the singular fortune of being born in a Barcelona apartment house built by Gaudí. His father said it looked like a rabbit hutch. This constituted Llorenz's first contact with art and rabbits. And it explains why he became an iconoclast in art and an expert in rabbits. From the conviction that he himself was a rabbit he drew the impetus that quickly turned him into the most springy of springboards in contemporary theater. Starting in his elastic youth, he gave such a kick to the stage that one doubts whether this art can ever again reach the heights to which he drove it. After Riber, no dramatic convention was violated that hadn't already been violated by him.

As is well known, the director was devoured by a lion near Fort Lamy in Chad on the 23rd of September 1958, in circumstances that continue to remain mysterious. From the collection of articles and essays *Homage à Llorenz Riber* (Plon, 1959), compiled on the anniversary of his death, we transcribe the following account of his appearance. It was first published in 1935 by the critic Enrique Martínez de la Hoz in a Barcelona daily. The director was very young at the time, and the critic rather hostile, but the testimony survives:

> Llorenz Riber arrives like an angel, lightly, teetering on the tips of his toes. His folded arms open, and he begins waving

his hands in harmony with the side-to-side flow of his long blond hair, straight and sleek. He is quite young, and yet he has already managed to make a name for himself among the worst directors in Spain. Instead of wearing his sweater under his jacket, he drapes it around his neck, boa-like, and whenever he flies into impatience at the incomprehension and stupidity of the world, he tosses a woolen sleeve over his shoulder, provoked, menacing as a viper.

A very different tone characterizes the critical essays that recall him in the 1940s and 1950s, the years when his maturity first erupted, cut short in such an annoying manner by the king of the beasts far from his lair (the lion was apparently a stray). From the above-mentioned *Homage* we have selected four particularly significant reviews, four moments in a career whose sole ambition was apparently digging the most original, scintillating graves for the theater. To complete our image of the prematurely eaten director, we append a most rare work from his reluctant ballpoint pen, the screenplay for a never produced film, a mixture of history and legend which bears the title of *Tristan and Isolde*.

Llorenz Riber

I
Tête de Chien (HOUND'S HEAD)
A play in three acts by Charles Rebmann
PETIT GAUMONT, VEVEY/ENTRE-DEUX-VILLES

Rumor has it that the director Llorenz Riber, for some unknown reason, habitually introduces one or more rabbits into his theatrical productions. He did it in his unforgettable staging of Maeterlinck's *Pelléas et Mélisande* at Poitiers, where Pelléas, dead at the end of the fourth act, reappeared at the beginning of the fifth, in the Gothic frame of a high castle window, dressed like one of Velázquez's *Meninas* with a huge stuffed rabbit in his arms. Then, at Ibiza, in Riber's version of *Doña Rosita la Soltera* (Mrs. Rosita, The Bachelorette), the rabbit was alive and served as a diversion for the female lead, who wheeled it around in a cage like a parrot.

In Victor Hugo's *Esmeralda,* the rabbit was a friar who, with two long furry ears dangling out of his hood, accompanied the Inquisitor Frollo everywhere. In Ghelderode's *Escurial,* the rabbit was dead, skinned and hung on a nail above the throne. In Riber's version of Sartre's *Huis Clos* (No Exit), a little boy dressed as a bunny carried a tray with cold drinks to the infernal guests. Unfortunately, nearly nobody saw it: the run was immediately halted at the author's request.

Not less unique was Riber's habit of mounting his most studied productions in places off the beaten track, like Caen, Arenys de Mar, Latina, La Valletta. He seems even to have done something in Tangiers. For the piece under review, he chose Vevey, or more exactly Entre-deux-Villes, exploiting the inauguration of a small but comfortable space in the new Petit Gaumont cinema.

Here we must allow ourselves an observation of a general character: does a theatrical work seem appropriate for inaugurating a movie house? The drama in question is a youthful yet presenescent work by our fellow citizen, Charles Rebmann. Hence, a great part of the audience came from Lausanne, but a segment also hailed from Geneva, another from Montreux. There was even a group of wealthy Italians, inexplicably noisy, who arrived on board a blue helicopter from Evian, where a conference on Marxist semantics was in progress.

A short walk from the cinema lies our beloved lake, made famous by Byron, gently lapping its age-old shores where the glossiest local fish dart frenetically among the stones (they are noticeably slimmer than those at Lausanne). Entitled *Tête de Chien,* Rebmann's drama in fact follows a Swiss family named Chien, although every character wears a papier-mâché or cloth mask in the shape of a rabbit's head. The action unfolds in Zurich at the home of Chien, a wealthy stockbroker.

One can immediately perceive that *Tête de Chien* isn't a work of the first rank, falling far short of the true and proper masterpieces to which Rebmann has accustomed us, especially the celebrated *Don Giovanni in Africa* of two years ago. The present work is unworthy even of a screenplay. The director has done his utmost, of course, but in such cases the text is best skipped entirely. We, at least, shall not speak of it. Notwithstanding this weak specimen, and despite the many charges of total incompetence now hurled at Rebmann from every quarter, he remains by far our most promising playwright.

The dialogue is heavy-going, comprising long interpolations from Patrice de La Tour du Pin and Roger Martin du Gard, sprinkled liberally with Maurice Merleau Ponty. It is enough to stop a wolf, attracted by all those fluffy white ears, from entering the auditorium. The second act opens with a discussion, apparently irrelevant, about the number of eggs that a Zurich blue-bottle can lay. In reality, however, the heated argument among the Chien children is like a brush fire in a mine field: it winds up exploding the rancor that accumulated during the first act. At this point, Riber's direction becomes indescribably brilliant. Although the action develops between the three walls of the same room, a parlor furnished in a contemporary style—lively, bright, and as threatening as a morning newspaper—such a small space couldn't yield more intelligent exits or more stunning entrances, more unexpected arrangements around (and beneath) the table, or more delicate variations on the struggle between the sunset and the electric light, which switched on and off intermittently, very different from natural light, yet in perfect harmony with the rise and fall of the voices. Suddenly, the situation becomes so unbearable that Nadine Chien (the stockbroker's wife, a rabbit as well, although the stepmother of the young Chiens) kills herself with a bullet to her shaggy forehead, using a small revolver inlaid with mother-of-pearl. The stage darkens, a long train clangs by, the lights finally return, and the surviving Chiens reappear with their real heads. Now that the tension is relaxed, the audience spits out fragments of gnawed fingernails and politely bursts into applause.

In the third act, everything is explicit. Shaken by the tragedy, the penitent Chiens feel the sting of doubt biting more deeply. Little by little, in a singularly unaffected way, the family's agitated discussion slips into the question of Palestine. The text, as we said, is better left unnoticed. Meanwhile huge butterflies of green and purple silk suspended from invisible nylon threads swarm onto the stage, flitting around the actors, producing the most elegant effect of a summer evening in Zurich in the district that faces the lake. The butterflies perch on the Chiens' noses, and the audience bursts into applause. A violent downpour is simulated at the window, accompanied by magnificent flashes of blue lightning. On the backcloth, they illuminate a large portrait of the rabbits' father, precisely the man they call "Tête de Chien." Llorenz Riber was summoned at least eight times to take a bow. For a director, a triumph in Switzerland is like being presented with a basket of eggs.

Claude Félon,
La Gazette de Lausanne

2

The Avant-garde under the Germans: The Couples' Embarrassment

The style of Feydeau—bourgeois couples hiding in closets—comes back into fashion. The style of Sartre—bourgeois couples hiding in offices—is now passé. Yet few recall the prophetic marriage of these two styles in the production of *L'embarras des couples,* staged in 1943 by the young director Llorenz Riber, beneath the German invaders' most inattentive gaze, in a little theater at Montreux (used today as the Center for Blood Collection).

L'embarras des couples was an adaptation, the work of Riber himself, made from a fairly obscure three-act comedy by an imitator of Feydeau, the prefect Jean Corgnol. The protagonists are two petty bourgeois couples, rather anonymously called Durand and Dupont. Perhaps to confer on his adaptation a certain *echt-deutsch* tone more agreeable to the authorities of the occupation, Riber replaced the protagonists' surnames with the much more suggestive Dachau and Auschwitz.

In those years, Paris was a difficult place to find actors willing to participate in an avant-garde experiment, the outcome of which, as imagined by the Catalan director, was probably uncertain. Drawing inspiration from this difficulty, Riber turned to the manager of a circus whose members had already been threatened repeatedly with deportation: they were offensive to the purity of the race. The director was especially impressed by a family of freaks. And from them he chose the most striking to serve as his actors: a one-eyed dwarf, the fattest woman in the world, a young girl with a yard-long beard, and Siamese twin brothers. To the brothers he assigned the part of Herr Dachau, whose wife was played by the bearded girl. The cyclopean dwarf and the fat lady formed the other couple, the Auschwitzs.

The play opens with the latter seated in the parlor, waiting for the Dachaus. The Auschwitzs have a young son who, however, is not entirely normal: in place of a human head he sports a frog's, although in other respects he can be called a typical boy (especially if seen from behind). All the same, his parents are quite worried about his future: he makes no progress and masturbates all the time, knee-deep in the garden pond. Where will they ever find a girl to marry him? With this end in mind, the Auschwitzs have published an advertisement in a newspaper, hoping to attract other parents with offspring as difficult as theirs. Female offspring, of course, since they possess a mindset typical of the Second Empire—irreverent, prankish, practical.

Only the Dachaus responded to the advertisement, and now the Auschwitzs impatiently await their arrival, passing the time with various conjectures about their future daughter-in-law's appearance.

"The important thing," observes Frau Auschwitz, "is that she be a healthy, respectable girl, even if she does have four breasts."

"Physical beauty is a burden," her husband adds, "that must be borne throughout one's life."

The Dachaus arrive. At first, their hosts fail to conceal their embarrassment at the fact that the new couple consists of three persons. But soon they adapt to the situation and manage to speak to the Herren Dachau as if they were a single gentleman.

"Our daughter Grenade," say the Dachaus, "is perfectly normal—except that she was born with a tortoise's head and it contains only a single hair."

"So does our son's!" exclaim the Auschwitzs in a paroxysm of delight.

The ice is broken, and the negotiations commence, full of promise.

Frau Dachau habitually strokes her beard with both hands before tossing it gracefully over her shoulder like a pheasant feather stole. She seems very attracted to Herr Auschwitz, who is so much more nimble and frolicsome than her husband. The one-eyed dwarf in turn looks favorably upon her. After a brilliant interlude of obscenely salacious repartee, he and the bearded woman leave for the Dachau home to inform the young Grenade of the agreement they have reached. Frau Auschwitz remains alone with the Dachau twins. The three-way conversation turns increasingly vulgar, almost Shakespearean, until the fat lady decides to confess her most burning curiosity: she wishes to see where and how the twins are joined.

Gallantly, the brothers start to undress. They slip off their jacket and step out of their trousers. When they are ready to take off their shirt, someone knocks at the door. General confusion. Desperate, Frau Auschwitz hides her boyfriends in a huge rosewood wardrobe and turns to open the door. It's the girl with the tortoise head. She explains that she has come at the command of her mother, who stayed at home with the little gentleman to scrutinize the question of the dowry—with three eyes, as it were. Bitten by sudden jealousy, the gargantuan Auschwitz grabs her hat and coat of Siberian wolf fur and dashes to the Dachaus', forgetting the boxer-clad chums she left in the wardrobe. End of first act.

In the second act, the boulevardier tradition prevails. Bonadieu Auschwitz and Grenade Dachau finally make one another's acquaintance, much to their mutual delight. All of a sudden, however, they begin to bicker. She boasts of her ability to keep her head underwater for hours; he demurs. A quarrel ensues, until they decide to stage a test in the bathtub. The two charming kids lock themselves in the bathroom. Worried about this turn of events, Grenade's fathers are on the brink of exiting the wardrobe when at that very moment the dwarf and the bearded woman reappear. The latter, having gotten wind of Frau Auschwitz's arrival from the peculiar scent of her fur, abscond by a window and hightail it over the roofs. The Herren Dachau hurriedly close the wardrobe door again. The adulterers, not finding anybody at home, believe themselves to be alone once more. But as soon as the dwarf, driven by another irrepressible wave of lust, starts to shimmy up the beard of his beautiful victim, the garden gate clangs. Frau Auschwitz is back. Terror-stricken, the one-eyed lothario shuts Frau Dachau in the bathroom, where she runs into Bonadieu, who is alone with his head underwater. Grenade left for the kitchen, where she is secretly eating her usual meal of lettuce.

Herr Auschwitz, in the meantime, found the Herren Dachau's trousers under a chair. He questions his wife who, declaring herself in the dark about everything, starts to suspect that he returned to the house with the bearded woman. So she slaps him, hoping to force his confession. Her suspicions are confirmed when she sees Frau Dachau leaving the bathroom, appalled that Bonadieu, believing her to be Grenade, rudely emptied his bladder down her back. The fat lady takes advantage of the resulting confusion to release the twins from the wardrobe. The intense excitement has transformed them into rabbits. Crestfallen, they allow themselves to be led to the kitchen, where they run into Grenade, who is virtually naked too, although entirely drenched. A violent scuffle erupts between the tortoise and the Siamese rabbits—over the lettuce. The act ends in pandemonium, everybody rushing about, swinging at each other, with the exception of Bonadieu who decides to stay in the bathtub forever.

The third act is much less busy. Grenade fills the kitchen sink and, disgusted by the adults' immorality, seats herself in it. The Herren Dachau, still rabbits clad in boxers, return to the wardrobe, and their wife locks them inside. Frau Auschwitz similarly packs her husband in a suitcase. Bonadieu is lying in the tub. The two ladies remain alone, so to speak. Frau Auschwitz, far too fat for this world, never intends to rise from her armchair. Frau Dachau likewise remarks on this vain agitation we call life. And in keeping with her pessimism, she cuts off her beard with a pair of scissors.

The other lady also takes up the scissors. Mournfully, the two good wives snip into strips the Herren Dachau's boxers. The twin rabbits wander around naked in the wardrobe and alternately utter melancholy comments on the weather, life on other planets, the death of the novel. Here one can observe Riber's adaptation deviating from Cargnol's original comedy, whose obtuse gaiety is many miles away from any concession to metaphysics. Gradually, the light turns lemon yellow. Every so often the dwarf thrashes around in the suitcase, and his wife slips him some lengths of cloth, one at a time, stuffing them through a little hole. The wardrobe, ominous in the fading light, emits the double crack of a revolver, followed by a thud, another thud, then silence. From the kitchen comes a cry, stifled, as if from a mouth held beneath a running tap; a similar cry comes from the bathroom, a dark response echoing in the woods. Finally, the shriek of a throttled boy is heard deep inside the suitcase. Yet the two sage wives continue, unperturbed, cutting cloth into shreds, all the cloth on the stage, whispering poems by Hugo von Hofmannsthal. In the occupied Paris of those years, the entire play acquired a vague air of defiance.

Valentin Rouleau,
Cahiers du Sud

3
The Search for the Self
Riber presents Wittgenstein

Last summer, when Llorenz Riber was summoned to Oxford to direct the dramatic adaptation of Wittgenstein's *Philosophical Investigations* (Blackwell), many believed it to be an all but hopeless undertaking. It was the first time that a renowned director attempted to dramatize a fundamental text of western philosophy—a text, moreover, that is the most modern, the most elusive, for some even the most profound in the tradition. To devise stage versions of the Socratic dialogues (as was done at the University of Bogotá) or certain voices in the Enlightenment *Encyclopedia* or Schopenhauer's *The World as Will and Representation* or even Plotinus's *Enneads* seemed not only possible, but desirable. Wittgenstein's masterwork, however, was a no go.

The first difficulty was the background music. Most people would have chosen Webern, almost automatically, since the composer and the philosopher reveal so many links and analogies, starting with the first letter of their surnames. But precisely for this reason, because the choice seemed so obvious, Riber wouldn't hear of it. Following his own peculiar taste, at once paradoxical and confident, he decided to use several of Beethoven's most famous quartets. After all, Beethoven also lived for years in Vienna. It was Beethoven, therefore, from beginning to end. Except for the Prologue, which, one will recall, opens with that remarkable passage from Augustine: "*Cum ipsi (majores homines) appellabant rem aliquam, et cum secundum eam vocem corpus ad aliquid movebant ...*" This was recited by Michael Lowry over an aria from Haydn's *Creation* (Haydn also lived in Vienna). Immediately after the Prologue came the Counterprologue, Nick Bates, who in a few words refuted the Augustinian thesis on the use of words. Then the action proper began.

The stage was bare, except for scattered suggestions of the immediate post-war period: rubbish, lost arts, a disemboweled alarm clock. First entered the Builder, who gave orders, then the Worker, who brought him building stones. "Slab!" said the Builder, and the other man brought him a slab. "Block," "beam," and the Worker responded. The game gradually expanded, becoming more complicated. New and strange words appeared, like "this" and "there," which were adequately clarified by the usual pointing gestures. Numbers were introduced (represented by letters of the alphabet) to indicate how many pieces of a given building material the Worker had to bring. Little by little the orders grew more complex. For example, "h-blocks-there."

The Builder grabbed a booklet of color samples that consisted of different colored squares. Whenever he gave an order, he pointed to one of the squares, and the Worker brought him slabs and blocks in that color. Thus, amidst the spirals of the second Razumovsky quartet, instead of constructing a building, the masons constructed a language. And whenever a new grammatical element was inserted into the game—a verb, an adverb, not to mention more complex words like "perhaps" or "even"—the audience, composed in great part of young linguistic analysts, applauded and whistled enthusiastically.

Reliable sources have asserted that Anscombe and Rhees also collaborated on the adaptation, which gave rise to unspoken yet irate disagreements. After the basic construction of language, a series of language-games followed. In addition to giving orders, these games, as listed by Wittgenstein himself, included describing the appearance of an object, or giving its measurements, reporting an event, speculating about an event, forming and testing a hypothesis, presenting the results of an experiment in tables and diagrams, making up a story and reading it, playacting, singing catches, guessing riddles, making a play on words, solving problems of æsthetics, translating from one language into another, asking, thanking, cursing, greeting, praying. The games formed a procession of very brief illustrative sketches that culminated in the moving apotheosis of the dictionary, carried on stage atop two Burmese elephants.

If the first act was entirely devoted to the construction of language, the second witnessed the construction of personality. That adorable sacred cow, Ruth Donovan, now took her turn in the limelight, playing a rather hysterical intellectual afflicted with persistent migraine, yet strangely convinced that her headache was located in another person's head, a German aunt brilliantly performed by Phyllis Ashenden. Donovan forced Ashenden to take aspirin with pyramidon and apply an ice bag to her forehead. She made her lay down and caressed her temples with a practiced, reassuring massage. And yet it was Donovan who constantly complained of headache. The act dwelt on other interesting illustrations of the theory of personality, until Donovan succumbed to the most delirious solipsism. She denied the existence of the other actors and the audience, did not respond when addressed, tried sitting but fell on the floor beside the chair, and was positively certain that the physical world had vanished. At this point, Ashenden, in a clear and convincing voice with a German accent, launched into the long refutation of solipsism that can be read in *The Blue and Brown Books,* still unpublished at the time but widely known in typescript (and not only to the adaptors). The act closed with a song of joy by Donovan, who rediscovered her self and others.

No brief description can possibly do justice to the third act of this memorable yet ephemeral production. A plethora of inventions, directorial as well as epistemological, packed the tiny Oxbridge stage with terse visual metaphors. Much of the act was obviously devoted to the charming elaboration of the "duckrabbit." This composite animal is so fashioned that if seen from one angle it looks like a rabbit, but if seen from another, it looks like a young duck. It constituted a vastly suggestive symbol, repeatedly adopted by the philosopher in the second and last part of the *Investigations* with the aim of clarifying—or obscuring—several controversial points regarding the theory of knowledge through sense perception.

Llorenz Riber is of course famous for loving rabbits. It was foreseeable that the need to introduce one so sophisticated as to seem both a rabbit and a farmyard bird would especially pique his intense vanity as an artist and illusionist. Indeed, this last act is nothing less than a prolonged tour de force of zoological fouettés, arabesques, pirouettes, and grands jetés, a complicated ballet based almost entirely on the elegant and ambiguous duck-rabbit. From a philosophical standpoint, it is true, the ballet itself doesn't land at any conclusion that can be called definitive. But neither does Wittgenstein's delightful last chapter.

Arthur O. Coppin,
The Observer

4
The Family Orsoli
Three identical acts with variations
BY LLORENZ RIBER

Llorenz Riber's brilliant, tenacious struggle against realism, especially against its conceptual degeneration into neorealism, is justly numbered among the most successful in recent years. One might say that it achieved its natural climax (or capsizing) with the version of *The Family Orsoli* that he conceived, wrote, and directed this winter at Teatro Santos Dumont in Bahia.

The utter novelty of *The Family Orsoli* consisted in the fact that every actor performing in the work actually belonged to the Orsoli family, a not very ancient clan of truck drivers from Ravenna. Sparing no expense, Riber traveled to Italy to select them in person. And then, sparing no expense, he had them transferred en masse to northeastern Brazil, along with all their moveables, household goods, furnishings. There they nightly enacted—before the astonished eyes of the Bahians (the poorest, most provincial, and most African Brazilians)—two hours chosen at random from the interesting but strenuous day of a normal Italian family.

Since the moment of reality chosen for fictive representation was supper, the television could not avoid being the principal protagonist. In fact, Riber was not less painstaking than Stanislavsky with the little details of the quotidian horror: he arranged to show several of the most characteristic programs that nourish an Italian family while they nourish themselves. The action opened, therefore, in the Orsoli's dining room-kitchen-parlor-foyer-study-den. They entered, sat at the table one after another, and without a second thought exchanged abuse, reproaches, kisses, and slaps while every head was turned toward the television. On the illuminated screen, a man who wore a deceptively cheerful expression spoke a deceptively sorrowful language, explaining—with suitable omissions—the latest developments in the recent coup d'état in Egypt.

The Orsoli gradually grew calm around a steaming bowl of pasta. At this point, no one could tear their eyes away from the screen—except mama, who attended to everybody's desires, pretending to satisfy them but only bringing frustration. Occasionally she lifted her gaze toward the appliance and blurted out: "How stupid!" As for father, every few minutes he resumed his ignored tale of what happened to a fellow truck driver last night. The man returned home from the tavern to find the dog poisoned on the doorstep, which made him worry that thieves were in the apartment, since his wife and children were visiting her aunt in Forlì. So first he rang the bell next door, and while he was explaining the situation to his neighbors, another dog arrived, his real dog, which meant that the dead one had to be his brother. So the man relaxed, entered his apartment, and in fact found no one inside. But Signor Orsoli never reached the end of this chilling story. The children shushed him because the TV was explaining how to breed chinchillas in the garden, you only had to live fifty thousand meters above sea level, and his daughter Giuliana flew into such a rage that she struck him on the head with a loaf of bread.

In the second act, the Orsoli family appeared in the same place, at the same hour, doing the same things as in the first act. Thus the play proceeded, each act exactly like the previous one. The audience started to fidget, protest, even threaten the actors and organizers in Portuguese, when suddenly the unforeseen occurred: the television broke. At first, the faces seemed distorted, more skewed than usual. Next, a series of dazzling flashes gaily crossed the screen from right to left and then immediately from left to right, like a rudder. They finally dissolved into blue-black darkness, which every so often flickered with the decomposed faces of girls, floating letters, and, most fleetingly, the American flag superimposed on a barren landscape scattered with scraggly sheep. The Orsoli could not swallow another mouthful. Mama despaired in dialect, and the children made all sorts of comments suitable to the situation, until father decided to break off his tale about the fraternal dogs and call his nephew, the TV repairman. Franco left, mama did her utmost to get the other children to eat something, Giuliana said she couldn't go on living in that house anymore, Enrichetto interjected a rather unpleasant remark about her fiancé, a quarrel erupted, and they traded insults, calling each other fascist or communist. The nephew arrived at just the right moment, and while ignoring the onlookers' profound silence, at once astonished and reverent, he started to fiddle with the television. An expert repairman, he quickly discovered the problem, the screen flickered with the frightful grimace of the same singer as before, her voice blaring, and the Orsoli family cleared away the table, although not without offering their courteous relative a small glass of carob wine.

The third act unfolded in the same place, at the same hour and with the same characters. The one change was the addition of Randazzo Benito, the Sicilian fiancé of the not so young Giuliana who in the previous act was declared to be a Mafioso by several of those present. The Orsolis' attitude changed from day to night. Mama continued to offer pasta to everyone, but now with a macabre smile fixed on her lips like a bewitching mask. The children continued complaining, but now in a low voice and with an unexpected surplus of good manners. Giuliana became almost kind, and beneath the table her fingers were interlocked with Randazzo's honest, excessively scrubbed fingers. All eyes stared at the screen, mama occasionally repeated, "Bravo!" and father wore glasses to see better, although with them he saw worse. The fiancé seemed very tired and yawned; he obviously worked the entire day. The others yawned in turn. The act ended with the television suddenly exploding and the arrival of a black rabbit from New Orleans, who dashed across the stage, exclaiming merrily: "Surprise! Surprise!"

Matteo Campanari,
Il Mondo

5
Tristan and Isolde
An Unpublished Screenplay by Lorenz Riber
SOURCE: MANUSCRIPT IN A PRIVATE COLLECTION

TIME: Middle Ages. PLACE: the English Channel and environs. Tristan, the son of Blancheflor, the sister of Mark of Cornwall, lives at the court of his uncle. He and Isolde, a medical student and Irish prince, the son of King Gurmun and Queen Lotte, are the cream of the *jeunesse dorée* in the period. They have long known many things about each other, but only from hearsay. Isolde considers Tristan—without ever having seen him—as the ideal folk singer: bushy blond beard, lion's whiskers, pink-tinted glasses. For Tristan, Isolde personifies a marvelous dream: a beardless university student from an excellent family.

Tristan owes the fame that surrounds him to his voice and his worthy customs: the precious legacy of his Breton blood. (His father, Rivalin of Parmenie, traveled from his native land to Tintagel, the seat of King Mark's court. The story of his amours with Blancheflor and the stag in the royal forest took a tragic turn.) He is undoubtedly the most handsome and athletic young man of his entire generation, the expert commander who rendered his uncle a thousand services—as a gym instructor in the cadet corps, as the brilliant and heroic horseman in so many polo matches, as the local chess champion. Yet he is also a most cultured individual in most uncultured times, a skilled speaker, versed in Spanish song and mass communications, possessed of a political mind. In other words, he isn't your typical playboy in the woods.

As for Isolde the Fair, his graces are joined to extraordinary spiritual gifts (his mother initiated him into the secrets of the kitchen, among others). And these are known to many travelers who have visited Ireland and its capital (Dublin). Yet few know how irresistible it is to weave the garlands of his praise.

Thus the two young men bear each other's image in their hearts, while their thoughts meet, overcoming every distance. (Opening shots.)

A personal encounter seems rather unlikely, however, since ancient enmity hopelessly separates Cornwall from Ireland, and the two countries have bitterly fought for many years with varying fortunes. Blood flowed in torrents, and the hatred was intense, perhaps greater on the Irish side: the law decreed that any Cornish man caught asking an Irish boy for little more than the time would be killed on the spot, his head hung on a lamppost.

At Tintagel, we find a strange situation in the royal castle. King Mark, upon the death of his wife Gerunda (renamed for the length and straightness of her nose), has designated his nephew as heir to the throne, a young man whom the monarch loves madly, and for this reason he does not wish to remarry. Those who frequent dens of ill repute whisper that he actually had his wife disemboweled for his nephew, since she got in the way of his affection. At court, however, among the mighty in the realm, many barons envy Tristan, plot against him, and entreat King Mark to name another heir who isn't so conspicuous.

Tristan, devoid of any egoism, is unconditionally faithful to Mark, so much so that he manages to confuse his fidelity with his interest in the fabled Isolde, wanting to conquer the young man by offering him as an heir to his lord. The plan does not lack political motives: beyond the advantages of having a doctor in the family, Tristan's gesture will serve to pacify the two countries, deeply afflicted with mutual hatred and devastated by a long war.

The scheme is bold, but seems unfeasible to the king when Tristan presents it to seek his advice. In the end, however, Mark surrenders to the idea, aiming to put a stop to the barons' impertinence. He is persuaded that he desires only Isolde. Yet if Tristan does not facilitate his rape of the Irish boy, the king will renounce the adoption and Tristan will remain heir to the throne.

The barons aim to make Tristan assume all the risks of the undertaking: they strive to persuade the king to send him to Ireland alone (with the secret hope that he won't return, capsized by the harsh Dublin law). Enraged, the king refuses and actually prefers to send the barons, so that Tristan might remain with him. Tristan, even though he finds it improbable that the unsanitary barons could seduce the student, demands the honor of the undertaking for himself. He allows only certain barons to accompany him and absolutely forbids them to touch the prey. Although worried, the barons unwillingly adapt themselves to the situation.

They depart. Near the Irish coast, the prince dons wretched, threadbare clothing, the most ragged blue jeans he can find, and climbs into a skiff with his harp and a huge rabbit for a gift. He commands the others to return to their fatherland and inform the king that he will promptly bring back Isolde for the adoption; otherwise he will never return. Then he lets the waves carry him toward the beach. The drifting boat is sighted by a coast guard patrol off Dublin and a rescue party sets out from the harbor.

A song greets the ears of the hastening sailors, accompanied by the sound of a harp, so sweet and enchanting that they all start dancing on deck, forgetting the oars and the rudder. They finally board the unguided skiff and find Tristan, who relates a tearful story. On a journey to Brittany with a wealthy companion and a precious cargo, he was surprised by pirates, who killed his companion and the ship's entire crew—except for the rabbit. Tristan was spared, together with the rabbit, although after being violated by them all, thanks to his masculine beauty and his songs. The more sympathetic pirates abandoned him on the boat in the middle of the sea with a modest store of victuals. He begs his rescuers for a fistful of grass, because the rabbit hasn't eaten anything since the day of the rape.

The Irish transport them both to land. While disembarking, he passes Isolde in the company of Brangane and his pages, returning from the summer castle (beach montage with Irish boys and young chaps in swimsuits, on water skis, nude against the sun, etc.). Many other people fly to the scene. Someone bears the news to the little prince, who commands that Tristan (now going by the name of Tantris) be immediately brought to court in order to sing and perform. The Englishman complies, and a great impression is made by his voice, his style, and his rabbit. In the end, Isolde has the castaways removed to the castle, lodging them in a tidy room where they might refresh themselves and get rid of the sea lice.

Thus Tristan comes to court under false pretense and quickly, with his muscles and talent, wins the favor of all, since he surpasses them in spirit, musical culture, and innate sense of publicity. Together with Isolde, he devotes himself to music and letters, rabbit breeding, chess. He also gives lessons in morality, judo, Spanish. In short, they are deeply in love with each other.

Yet when reminded of his mission and his duty to King Mark, Tristan represses this feeling, even though it is more than natural between two handsome, rich, athletic young men. When he realizes his love for Isolde, he brightens, because he thinks that the prince will follow him most gladly to Cornwall.

Isolde, for his part, lives with the anxiety that his penchant is not based on terra firma. Ever since learning that the poor, unknown, yet fascinating merchant-troubadour sleeps with his rabbit, he worries that his affection may not be fully requited.

Tristan finally reveals his true identity to him. It is a scene rich with conflicting sentiments. Isolde thus comes to know that his beloved is Tristan: the young man who was once no more than a name and a dream has cunningly arrived to win him. Yet not for himself, but for King Mark. Must he follow Tristan only to wind up in his uncle's arms?

In the name of Mark and his political projects, Tristan tries to convince Isolde with the vehemence of his expert tongue. He ultimately obtains the boy's consent, now conquered by the mirage of a ménage à trois with a royal participant. Everything, or nearly everything, is disclosed to his venerable parents. And the revelations are followed by surprise, anger, reflection, joy—hence agreement. Tristan grabs the rabbit and leads Isolde to Cornwall.

During the voyage, a strange situation emerges on board the ship. Isolde, whom till now no one has ever refused, is insanely jealous of the rabbit and wavers between love and hate. Tristan, in contrast, wavers between the call of instinct and reasons of state. But one night, alone, after everyone else has gone ashore, the two young men drink a liter of Irish beer, and Isolde's lust combusts spontaneously, no holds barred. The rabbit is banished to the hold beneath the poop deck, and the two princes lodge together for the rest of the journey, scared shitless of the undesired end.

King Mark welcomes them with great pomp and names Isolde his heir. That very night, when the adoption is about to go into effect, the obliging Brangane allows himself to be convinced by the other two: he substitutes for Isolde in the family bed, and Mark spends the rest of the night with him.

The ruse continues without Mark's knowledge because Tristan enjoys free access to Isolde's rooms, and they manage to avoid arousing any suspicion. But their happiness, born under the bad sign of fatality, is discovered by Marjodoc, the king's steward, who himself burns with lust for Isolde.

For years Marjodoc habitually slept in the same tent with the rabbit and Tristan. Hence, he quickly notices that every night at the same hour Tristan steals into the rooms of the princely heir. Marjodoc follows his tracks in the snow and discovers Tristan and Isolde playing chess on a carpet, despite the faithful Brangane's attempt to cover the lamp with the chessboard.

Pain and rage! Marjodoc, however, does not inform the king that he discovered them engaged in a pushy Indian gambit, although he does report certain rumors, sowing unrest while staying on his guard.

Terrible doubts assail Mark because the rumors hit so close to home, involving his own son, pure as an angel, and his dearest friend and nephew, not so pure but still family.

The king and Marjodoc, gnawed by suspicion, hire the dwarf Melot as a spy. The dwarf is a failure at spying: on his first observation he sends for Mark, but the others spot him in sufficient time to pretend that they were playing chess in a tree. Mark, enraged, hurls the dwarf into the river. Then he returns to court and orders that the two young men be banished. The word is given out that they went to France to play chess.

The two princes take refuge in the forest, living in a cave, ancient sanctuary of giants (montage of the serenely pastoral life at the height of the Middle Ages amidst the beasts in the woods). The king has followed them, sad to say, and discovers them in the cave, intent on the final move in a particularly difficult game, tower against tower, on the rabbit's straw bed. The two protest that everyone in Ireland plays chess in the Middle Ages.

But the king won't stay to hear reasons. He unsheathes his broad sword and flings himself at Tristan. In a desperate attempt to save his friend—who, instead of flinching, bares his breast to the blade—Isolde steps between them. As a result, both young men are impaled on the same weapon, which penetrates deeply into the rock. Conjoined like two thrushes on the bloody spit of death, Tristan and Isolde manage to detach themselves from the rock, take a few steps together, and finally fall lifeless across the chessboard. Whereupon the rabbit turns ferocious, flings himself at the king, and devours him.

Reprinted through the kindness of
Charles Guy Fulke Greville,
count of Warwick

Alfred William Lawson

In the 1940s, in the state of Iowa, near Des Moines, a university existed where the curriculum focused exclusively on the teachings of a single person: Alfred William Lawson, its owner.

Supreme Head and first "Knowlegian" of the University of Lawsonomy, Lawson described himself in his book *Manlife* (1923), written under the pseudonym of Cy Q. Faunce and devoted entirely to documenting his own intellectual feats in these terms:

> There seems to be no limit to the depth of his mental activities.... Countless human minds will be strengthened and kept busy for thousands of years developing the limitless branches that emanate from the trunk and roots of the greatest tree of wisdom ever nurtured by the human race.

On the book jacket, the publisher (who was Lawson himself) paid respectful homage to the author: "In comparison to Lawson's Law of Penetrability and Zigzag-and-Swirl movement, Newton's law of gravitation is but a primer lesson, and the lessons of Copernicus and Galileo are but infinitesimal grains of knowledge."

"The birth of Lawson was the most momentous occurrence since the birth of mankind," Lawson immodestly observed. This event took place in London on the 24th of March 1869. After moving to Detroit with his parents, the scholar made his first key scientific discovery at the age of four: he "noticed that when he used the Pressure from his lungs to blow the dust within his bedroom, it moved away from him, and when he used the Suction of his lungs by drawing in his breath, the dust was moved toward him." From this phenomenon he derived his chief insight into the two elementary principles that govern the movement of the universe: Suction and Pressure.

Lawson ran away from home, worked at various trades, and at the age of nineteen became a professional baseball player. In 1904, he published a utopian narrative, *Born Again,* which one reviewer judged the worst work of fiction in the world. In his autobiography, however, Lawson revealed that "many people consider it the greatest novel ever written by man." The novel relates, in a repetitive and digressive fashion, how the author managed to give up the vice of smoking. It was translated into German, French, Italian, and Japanese.

After publishing the novel, Lawson dedicated himself to aviation and founded the Lawson Aircraft Corporation. Between 1908 and 1914 he published two popular aeronautical magazines, *Fly* and *Aircraft.* It was in fact he who coined the word *aircraft,* literally "air boat," which today is synonymous with *airship* in English. He introduced it into the dictionary when he worked as editor of the aviation entries in an edition of *Webster's.* In 1919, he invented, designed, and constructed the first passenger airplane. In 1921, one of his planes crashed. Lawson then retired from the aviation industry to dedicate himself to sociology, creating the Humanity Benefactor Foundation based in Detroit.

Suddenly he became rich and famous, thanks to a new economic cult of his invention: the Direct Credits Society. To illustrate his system of direct credit, Lawson published two volumes, the first in 1931, *Direct Credits for Everybody,* the second in 1937, *Know Business.* The author proposed the abolition of capital and the suppression of interest. These two measures alone were deemed sufficient to free the world from the tyranny of money and speculators. The cult published a magazine called *Benefactor,* which claimed to reach a circulation of seven million overnight. The Direct Credits Society in turn attracted supporters in the tens of thousands. At their mass rallies, they wore white uniforms with diagonal red sashes.

On the 1st of October 1933, Lawson spoke for two hours to sixteen thousand people who gathered at the Olympian auditorium in Detroit. At the close of the demonstration, the group sang in unison a hymn composed for the occasion (by Lawson, no doubt) where each stanza ended with the refrain:

> Alfred William Lawson
> is the greatest don
> God bestowed on man.

In 1942, now a very wealthy man of sixty-three, Lawson purchased a vast complex of academic buildings, closed since 1929, to house the University of Lawsonomy. The only texts admitted in the new university were the owner's writings. The professors at Lawsonomy were called "Knowlegians," and the highest Knowlegians, Generals. The courses were free. The university drew a great part of its funding from the resale of war surplus materials—a practice that got Lawson called to testify before the Senate Small Business Committee in 1952. Since the first Knowlegian nurtured an intense hatred of cigarettes and smoke in general, he had the chimney of the heating system demolished. Thenceforth the smoke was diverted away from campus, shot through pipes and underground tunnels.

Students were not permitted to eat meat. A daily salad was required. "All salads should contain a sprinkling of freshly cut grass." Students had to sleep nude, and on waking they were forced to immerse their heads in cold water. Kissing was forbidden within the perimeter of the university to prevent the spread of microbes. This monastic asceticism appeared to compensate in part for the iconoclasm of the course material.

Lawson defined Lawsonomy as "the knowledge of Life and everything pertaining thereto." The student of Lawsonomy must renounce all the officially recognized sciences, which are held to be frivolous lies. "The basic principles of physics were unknown until established by Lawson," explains Lawson.

Energy, to start with, doesn't exist. The universe consists only of substances with greater or lesser density, which move according to the two elementary Lawsonian principles already noted: Suction and Pressure. These principles constitute the foundation for the Law of Penetrability and are efficaciously complemented by the important third principle, Zigzag-and-Swirl, which determines the movement of every molecule. To study these immensely complicated movements, Lawson proposes the creation *ab initio* of a completely new "Supreme Mathematics."

The entire world is governed by Suction and Pressure. Light is a "substance drawn into the eye by Suction," just as sound is sucked into the ear. The force of gravity is simply the "pull of the earth's Suction." In the light of the Lawsonian laws, "all problems theoretically concocted in connection with Physics will fade away." In the field of physiology too: air is sucked into the lungs, food into the stomach, blood through the limbs. Our excretions, however, are due to pressure. The vital swirl subsists as long as the internal suction and pressure are balanced. No sooner is the balance destroyed than the swirl ceases and death supervenes.

Even the earth obeys the two principles. Through the ether circulates a substance of even rarer density, "Lesether," or Lawson's ether. The difference in pressure between the ether and Lesether causes a powerful suction which collects at an opening near the North Pole. A long tube perforates the earth axially. From it branch the arteries that give life to all parts of the planetary organism, as well as the veins that flush away waste matter. The South Pole is the anus of the earth, from which the "discharged gases" are eliminated by simple pressure.

Not unexpectedly, sex in both humans and animals is regulated by suction and pressure. "Suction is the female of movement, pressure the male." Magnetism is simply a low-grade form of sexual attraction. The brain is inhabited by tiny creatures called "Menorgs" (from "mental organizers"), who are assigned the task of directing mental operations. "To move your arm requires the concentrated efforts of billions of Menorgs working together under orders from one little Menorg." The brain is also the seat of the "Disorgs," or disorganizers, "microscopic vermin that infect the cells of the mental system and destroy the mental instruments constructed and operated by the Menorgs."

Since Lawson refused to pay taxes, the Internal Revenue Service forced him to auction off the university in 1954. It was bought by a Detroit businessman for $250,000 and later transformed into a shopping mall.

Jesús Pica Planas

The inventor, in the modern sense of the word, is an invention of the nineteenth century. And like all nineteenth-century things, he reaches perfection in the twentieth. The professional inventor is a man—rarely a woman—dedicated to the design and construction of devices that are striking in their uselessness. Patent Offices preserve memorable examples, such as a contraption for men to lift their hats without hands when a woman passes. Perhaps the most fertile of inventors, as well as the most useless, was Jesús Pica Planas, a native of Las Palmas in the Canary Islands.

Facing an always benevolent sea, beneath a sky that is worryingly the same from January to December, his back to a boring city that observes the passing world unaffected, Pica Planas planned his projects. On a few occasions, they even attained a material form. Between 1922 and 1954, the year of his death, not far from the unimpressive little church where Columbus prayed before departing for America, perched on a patio amidst blue tiles, carnations, sinuous cats, and flitting cochineal, the inventor invented:

A complete system of pantographs, prehensile and self-propelled, to enable a priest to celebrate the Mass by himself.

A mousetrap in the form of a guillotine operated by photoelectric cell. To be placed in front of holes.

A steam-driven piano, similar in every way to a pianola, activated by a gas compressor installed in place of the pedals.

A wind clock, using a standard windmill, appropriate for lighthouses, high mountains, and other inhospitable places.

A stove that functions on rubbish, waste paper, offal, leftovers.

A bicycle with slightly elliptical wheels to mimic the pleasant gait of a horse.

A curved funnel to plant radishes with remarkable efficiency.

A collapsible, bell-shaped tent with an opening to accommodate the head: for undressing on the beach without being seen.

An electrical appliance with a bell to signal when the tap hasn't been closed properly.

A washing machine operated by treadle, later superseded by an internal combustion engine.

A specially grooved plate for eating asparagus.

An anti-theft wallet with a chain and padlock.

A cooling system wherein a sprinkler set into the window frame douses the blinds and shutters with a continuous jet of water.

Elastic air-tight panties for bitches in heat.

A new type of wooden pliers to pick up fallen or shaky high-tension lines.

A beach robe with a heater that runs on a manually operated, high friction gravel grinder. The heat is conducted from the grinder to the robe through a network of rubber tubes.

A candlestick for honoring sacred images, in which the candles are set on a wheel turned by a clockwork mechanism with a guaranteed duration of forty-two hours.

A secret chemical weapon consisting of a blowgun and darts trimmed with tiny vials of prussic acid.

A push-button cigarette case that dispenses cigarettes one at a time, lit.

A total silencer for airplanes, based on the principle of quilting.

A pistol that shoots artificial flowers made of cloth and paper, a party favor for Carnival.

A multiple telephone that enables friendly, diverting conversations among twenty-five people.

An electric clock connected to a scintillator which emits a spark every fifteen minutes to warn of violent explosions in case of a gas leak. The entire explosion is thus subdivided into thirty or forty small ones of no consequence.

A selective system of bells to distinguish whether the person at the door is an important visitor, somebody insignificant, a nuisance, or the mail.

A walking stick with a step counter installed in an ornamental handle: whenever the stick touches the ground, the counter clicks.

A pair of shoes with a step counter, idem.

An automatic, steam-driven chicken plucker, adaptable to turkeys.

A perpetual calendar in the shape of a rotating sphere, a meter and a half in diameter.

A writing desk with twelve shelves arranged like an amphitheater.

A broiling spit with an engine that runs on gas, wood, and sawdust, later superseded by a wheel of multiple spits turned by four tortoises.

A pair of eyeglasses with rearview mirrors in each corner to enable the wearer to see if somebody is following without turning the head.

An automatic card shuffler and dealer.

A small rotary press powered by children riding one or more seesaws.

A ring-shaped swimming pool built with different water levels and functioning locks in order to breed salmon at home.

A water pump for a hotel connected to the revolving door at the entrance, operated without charge by the guests.

A glass-topped funeral limousine with a white or blue interior to amuse patients from hospitals and insane asylums by driving them down the principal street in Las Palmas and other panoramic places.

A polarized binocular for solar eclipses.

A pneumatic underwater postal service between Las Palmas and Santa Cruz in Tenerife.

An anti-theft device that squirts the thief with a violent jet of green paint, indelible and extremely foul-smelling.

A dining room table with fins or projections on which to rest the elbows.

A lightning rod to be mounted on the heads of grazing livestock.

A network of buoys fitted with an automatic alarm to announce the approach of a school of sardines.

Wave-powered bellows set atop pedestals on a barge of beaten copper or rubber (about one meter in diameter).

An inkwell for inks in five different colors—red, green, yellow, blue, purple—for writing artistic manuscripts or facetious letters.

A two-sided band saw powered by a Halladay wind engine.

A high-speed Carborundum grinding wheel placed inside safes and strong boxes for cutting off the hands of thieves.

An economical paste or mortar made from animal bones (from cattle, horses, sheep, chicken, and fish) for paving roads.

A new kind of bottle with two corks—one at the top, the other at the bottom—to facilitate washing.

A steam-driven bus.

A secret military code linked to the daily lottery drawing.

A new type of travel wig that is attached, not to the head, but to the brim of a hat, at once decorative and dashing.

A safety elevator with doors on four sides, manually operated by rack and pinion, equipped with an internal brake that utilizes wedges or bars in case the cable should snap.

A toothpaste made from rue to combat the vice of smoking.

A button-holing machine for emergencies, mounted on rust-proof metal clamps.

A toilet for every age with a hand-operated hydraulic press to lower and raise the seat to the proper height.

A hot-air balloon designed for fishing on the surface of the water with a trawl.

An anti-noise device for enamored cats, lined throughout in cork and asbestos.

A portable bridge composed of perforated aluminum, extremely light, capable of being set up automatically by a single person and carried in a backpack.

A propeller-powered bus.

A tandem bicycle for five people, hinged, suitable for routes with sharp turns.

A little centrifugal condenser for the table to blend oil and vinegar and distribute it over the salad.

A fan with a sufficiently focused airflow to wave the national flag on windless days.

A sewing machine driven by waterwheel at low tide.

A heat accumulator, comprising a single block of material with a high melting point, one meter square, placed in the center of the room and heated during the day by a coal stove underneath.

A musical water meter for eddying currents.

A disinfectant sharpener to restore the tips of used toothpicks.

A gauge to check periodically the diameter and circumference of lampshades.

A pair of shears whose cutting edges are adjusted by gravity for use in surgical procedures (amputations, etc.).

A new type of lightning-proof screen consisting of two upholstered sheets of plywood stuffed with paramagnetic iron shavings.

A drill with a soft bit for dentists.

A mortised extruder with a runner adjusted by rack and pinion or nut and bolt to shape tagliatelle and other varieties of dried pasta according to the Italian taste.

A metal mosquito net ventilated internally, suspended on pulleys with swivel supporting arms connected to an alarm or carillon.

A steam-driven funeral crane, camouflaged as an angel, archangel, or St. Christopher, to lower or lift a coffin into a grave or niche.

A propeller-driven ferryboat with one rudder (to reduce friction).

An automobile made almost entirely of rubber to withstand accidents.

A blast furnace for the garden to profit from the disposal of tin cans, aluminum foil, and scrap iron.

A switch that can be connected to a foot to avoid falling asleep without turning off the light.

A perpetual motion device, operated by a set of cannon balls that ingeniously, through the force of gravity, turn a waterwheel composed of iron spoons. The whole thing is to be immersed in extra virgin olive oil.

Félicien Raegge

On the deserted streets of Geneva, Félicien Raegge intuited the reversible nature of time. A tag taken from Helvetius, undoubtedly unoriginal, furnished the key: "We are the ancients." The fact that by tacit accord nearly all thinkers and scholars joined in calling the first humans "ancient"—including the very first, Palaeonthropus—and reserved "modern" for our dusty, decrepit contemporary specimens meant only one thing: time on earth, human time, runs opposite to what everyday parlance would lead us to believe. That is to say, backward, from present to past, from future to present.

The Englishman Dunn, the Spaniard Unamuno, and the Bohemian Kerça already alluded to this reversal. From it, Unamuno derived a striking metaphor for a sonnet; Kerça devised a comedy that begins with the end and ends with the beginning; and Dunn inferred a basic idea in oneiromancy, that dreams are in reality memories of a future that already happened. On this theme the English thinker had already written a treatise, which won the assent of many—but never fully convinced anyone. He argued that the true destiny of every man is to become a baby, the days of the wise rush toward ignorance, and since so-called memories of the past are nothing more than dreams, the only real dreams, we cannot know with certitude who we are, nor when we were born, because we are yet to be born.

These and other speculators who approached the theme have barely grazed it, so to speak, only to keep at a judicious remove afterward, troubled by the scant feasibility of its consequences. Or they immersed themselves as if venturing into a swamp, bound to terra firma by rope and winches, capable of withdrawing at the opportune moment. No author of a pertinent essay or book wrote it with the sincere conviction that they were erasing a text that had existed for centuries, aiming solely to make it vanish from circulation. And none of these authors found themselves several months younger or several experiences poorer than before. Which would have happened if time ran backward. Raegge, however, is distinguished precisely by the depth of his conviction: he completely accepted the consequences of his own theory and lived according to its implications.

Theories are not formulated without the will to communicate them. Human, all too human, Félicien Raegge also composed a book, which was foreseeably entitled *La fléche du temps* (The Arrow of Time), but less foreseeably published at Grenoble in 1934. Yet, if truth be told, he was very much aware of annulling irrevocably the best explanation ever offered for the retrograde character of time. He took comfort, he insinuates, in the idea that all ideas were destined to disappear. He needed only await the moment of their emergence; an instant later, in the backward flow of centuries, the idea began to fade. Man will become truly ancient, will reach the stage of banal magic, and finally one day find himself mute, perhaps growling.

Almost inevitably, the reversal of time carries a species of determinism. If the dream of what we call the past is a true dream, most of what will happen is known. Beneath the bust of Pompey, the swords of the noted conspirators will issue from a corpse's twenty-three wounds; speaking Latin in reverse, the dead man will converse with Cicero. Other events will unfold with even greater precision. Since Shakespeare's tragedies now exist, one day in London a man who is increasingly unknown must abolish them, individually, from end to beginning, with a pen. Thereafter the theater will be a different, much poorer art. On another day, still remote, someone will rise from the tomb of Theodoric and live as king of Italy for a time, until it conquers (loses) him.

Raegge's book is devoted to these examples and many others of the same ilk. The book is at once coherent and honest. On the future it doesn't have much to say, since the future is the immense unknown mass of what has already happened, which the present wipes away like a sponge. When the sponge reaches the past, it too will be wiped away. The ultimate destiny of man is primigenial perfection, the mindless babble at the dawn of creation. Near the end of his book, the author doesn't fail to observe that reversing the arrow of time neither adds or removes one iota from the temporal universe—which we too know and perceive. As Wittgenstein later wrote (as he had already written), "Call it a dream. It does not change anything."

Author's Note

Nearly all the details mentioned in connection with Babson, Lawson, and Hörbiger are drawn from Martin Gardner's collection, *In the Name of Science* (New York: Dover, 1952). Littlefield, Carroll, Kinnaman, Piazzi-Smyth, Lust, and the advocates of the hollow earth theory spring from the same source. Carlo Olgiati is the author's great-grandfather. Armando Aprile is actually named after a well-known publisher of books on pedagogy. The director Llorenz Riber is not to be confused with the poet from Majorca who bears the same name.

Translator's Acknowledgments

I was aided by a number of publishers and editors, friends and colleagues. Many years ago Kristin Jarratt introduced me to the wonders of Wilcock. Earlier versions of several chapters were printed by Seth Frechie and Andrew Mossin (*To*), Teresa Leo (*Painted Bride Quarterly*), Bradford Morrow (*Conjunctions*), and Eliot Weinberger (*Sulfur*). Eliot suggested the rendering of the title and called my attention to a Wilcock dossier in the Buenos Aires magazine *Diario de Poesía* (no. 35, October 1995). Amanda Zamuner was able to get me a copy of it. This dossier is the source of the biographical details given in the first chapter. Translating a writer with an Argentine past led me to consult with several accomplished translators of Latin American writing: Suzanne Jill Levine, Carol Maier, and Esther Allen. Francesca Sintini of the Italian publisher Adelphi kindly sent me a number of Wilcock's books. My work was supported in part by a Summer Research Fellowship from Temple University, for which I was recommended by Daniel O'Hara and Philip Stevick.

Tom Christensen encouraged this project over several years and accepted it for publication. Kirsten Janene-Nelson of Mercury House shepherded the manuscript through the press and beyond with her customary resourcefulness and enthusiasm.

The illustrations are reprinted here courtesy of the Charles L. Blockson Afro-American Collection and the Paskow Science

Translator's Acknowledgments

Fiction Collection, both at Temple University. I owe a special thanks to Charles Blockson and Thomas Whitehead for giving me access to these materials.

For their computer expertise, I thank Chris Benham, Matthew A. Palladinetti, and Greg Szczepanek.

Gemma Venuti maintained a suitably surreal atmosphere while I wrote the translation. Julius, who arrived before for the final revision, raised an iconoclastic racket in the background. Lindsay Davies provided uninterrupted stretches of time—a most tangible form of inspiration.

About the author

Born in Buenos Aires into a family with distant Spanish connections, JUAN RODOLFO WILCOCK (1919-78) was the only child of an English father and an Italian mother. He learned Spanish in London, English and Italian in Argentina. In the 1940s he joined the circle of innovative writers that included Jorge Luis Borges, Adolfo Bioy Casares, and Silvina Ocampo. In Spanish he wrote existentialist parables and symbolist poetry with a homoerotic subtext.

Repulsed by Juan Perón's dictatorship (1946-55), Wilcock traveled abroad, searching for a congenial place to stage an exile. Wilcock landed in Rome, and from 1960 to his death in 1978 he became a leading Italian writer, a friend of Alberto Moravia, Elsa Morante, and Pier Paolo Pasolini. He published some fifteen Italian books: poetry, drama, journalism, and fiction. He also authored many literary translations into Italian, working from English, French, and Spanish, rendering a dazzling array of works from Shakespeare and Christopher Marlowe to Joyce and Woolf to Genet and Borges.

About the translator

LAWRENCE VENUTI is a distinguished translator of Italian literature as well as an internationally known translation theorist and
historian. Recent translations include I.U. Tarchetti's *Fantastic
Tales* and *Passion: A Novel*, both for Mercury House. Venuti has
illuminated the practice of translating in such books as *The
Translator's Invisibility* and *The Scandals of Translation*. His translations have received awards and grants from PEN American
Center, the NEA, and the NEH. Formerly a Fulbright lecturer
in translation studies, he has also served as a judge for the PEN-
BOMC Translation Award and the Modern Language Association's Scaglione Prize for Literary Translation. He is currently
professor of English at Temple University.